WITCH ORACLE IN WESTERHAM

Paranormal Investigation Bureau #8

DIONNE LISTER

Copyright © 2019 by Dionne Lister

ISBN 978-0-9946025-8-9

Cover art by Robert Baird

Content edit by Becky at Hot Tree Editing

Line edit by Chryse Wymer

Proofreading Mandy at Hot Tree Editing

All rights reserved.

Paperback edition.

 Created with Vellum

To Izzy and Lily, you'll never read this book because you're cats, but thanks for keeping my lap warm and for being soft and cuddly. Okay, yes, I'm scraping the bottom of the barrel with dedications now. Seriously, writing eight books in thirteen months, I'm running out of people I even know at this point.

CHAPTER 1

*O*h. *My. God.* I stood and stared, mouth agape. Excitement made me squee a little. "Oh my God. Oh my God. Oh my God." I squeed again. Amongst the twinkling lights, tinsel, and trees adorned with all manner of bright baubles stood the Christmas tree of my dreams. The tree I never knew I needed. There was only one thing that could elicit such a loss of blabber control towards a Christmas tree, and that was… squirrels!

Peering from the green branches were squirrels of every description: furry brown ones with a dusting of snow on their noses, golden ones, ones with red and white scarves and Santa hats, squirrels holding tiny presents in their little paws, a squirrel holding teeny pine cones, and my favourite, one with adorable, minuscule red deer antlers on its head.

My grin hurt my cheeks. Will shook his head. "You're a

nutter. No wonder you feel such an affinity towards tree rats."

I narrowed my eyes at him. "Insult my spirit animal again, and there'll be no Christmas present for you in two weeks."

He smiled, flashing his dimples, and pulled me to him. "That's okay. I already got what I wanted." Gah, how could I argue with that? Beren and Liv exchanged an "oh, how sweet" look. I sighed, defeated. I was torn between being disappointed I wasn't going to win and delighted he loved me. Who was I kidding? Will loved me. It didn't get any better than that.

"I wonder if Angelica would let me make a squirrel tree for the lounge room?"

Liv tilted her head, eyeballing the tree. "Hmm, maybe not. I'm sure she'd be okay with a couple of squirrels, though." Liv turned to a golden-coloured tree with golden baubles and gold-coloured tinsel. "I love this one. So pretty."

"It's rather… gold." They'd gone overboard with their theme, but in this display, anything went. We were in St Mary's Church Westerham for their annual Christmas Tree Festival. Anyone could display their tree, and tonight, there were over one hundred, according to one enthusiastic woman we'd overheard earlier. They twinkled and sparkled in the muted light, surrounded by stained-glass windows darkened by night. Loud murmuring rose over a background of Christmas carols piped in through speakers.

"Mine's better!"

"No, mine is, you mouldy crumpet-eating goat's teat." Wow, that was imaginative.

We all turned towards the commotion. Two men faced off in front of two trees, trees that looked fairly similar. The hairs on the back of my neck stood on end, and I shivered. It was almost the feeling of magic but was extremely subtle. It was probably just a gust of cold air—old churches were draughty, especially in winter.

"Who you calling a goat's teat?" The taller man shoved the shorter man, sending him flying into one of the trees—I had no idea whose tree was whose. He crashed into it, sending red and blue glass baubles smashing to the stone church floor. So much for the Christmas spirit. Despite the tree's sturdy base, it toppled backwards.

"Watch out!" a lady yelled.

Someone else screamed.

The tree fell with a whoosh, thud, and tinkle—a combination of sounds I never thought I'd hear. The man who'd pushed the other stood glaring at his adversary who was disentangling himself from the mess and trying to stand.

A woman called out, "There's an old lady trapped under the tree!"

Will and Beren raced over, pushing past the crowd that was uselessly standing there staring, unsure what to do. Beren helped the man get up, then helped Will lift the tree off the woman and to the side. The frame supporting it had broken—that tree wasn't going back up. The shorter man ran at the taller one and shoulder-charged him, knocking him to the ground. Liv and I looked at each other, eyes wide.

"Are you going to do anything?" she asked.

"Nope. That tall guy's a pig. He ruined the other man's tree. Did you see the look on the shorter guy's face? I think he deserves some kind of revenge."

She nodded, a thoughtful expression on her face. "Makes sense."

The priest and another woman in a red outfit who had a name tag on, so probably worked at the church in some capacity, hurried past to help Will and Beren. *Oh.* I frowned. Will breathed into the woman's mouth while Beren performed chest compressions. The warmth of magic flowed from him. Was he healing her or just trying to see what was wrong?

The woman in the red outfit pulled a phone out of her bag and called an ambulance. Someone started sobbing loud enough that it echoed in the now-silent church. Even the two idiots who'd been fighting over their Christmas trees had stopped pummelling each other, probably realising what had happened.

Will and Beren kept up the CPR as sirens wailed closer, but the warmth of Beren's magic cut off, leaving me cold. She obviously wasn't going to make it. I turned to Liv and shook my head. Her face registered shock, and her eyes glistened with tears. "I know," I whispered, my voice almost breaking. That poor woman's family—to lose her in such a stupid way, and just before Christmas. There wouldn't be any celebrating for them.

That thought led to painful ones about my parents and all the years I'd missed celebrating with them. James, my brother, had done his best to make sure all our Christmases were special, but there was no way he could bring our parents back, so as much as we acknowledged the holiday and exchanged presents, we always did so with heavy hearts. I sighed.

Two paramedics ran through the door. After a quick chat to Will, they took over, and the boys joined Liv and me. Two police officers weren't far behind the ambos, and they started off their investigation by talking to the priest.

I looked up at Will. "Will the tall guy get charged with manslaughter?"

"Maybe. But it's nothing to do with us now." He lowered his voice to a whisper. "None of them are like *us*, so it'll go through the normal channels."

By *us*, he meant witches. The PIB handled witch-related crimes—whether a witch was the victim or the perpetrator or both. The PIB was always busy, unfortunately, so it was good the normal police were going to deal with this. The ambulance officers had assessed the patient and were performing CPR, but I knew it wasn't going to help—if Beren's magic couldn't help, nothing could. It was time to go. "I don't know about you guys, but I'm not really in the mood to look at any more trees."

"Agreed," said Will, while Liv and Beren nodded. Will grabbed my hand. "Let's go." My stomach still did little flips whenever he touched me, and I couldn't deny the comfort the warmth of his touch gave me now. As we walked past the sad scene, I couldn't help looking at the old lady. The parts of her face I could see were whiter than a new piece of paper—the ambos had a plastic mask on her face and were pumping it to make her breathe. I had a new appreciation for the job they had. It must be so fulfilling to save lives, but many times, they lost their patient. What a burden to bear. How did you watch a patient die, then go home and be happy in front of your kids? I whispered, "Thank you" as I passed.

When we made it outside, the frigid air slapped all sadness away—I couldn't concentrate on anything but how cold my nose and cheeks were. I shoved my free hand in my jacket pocket. "It's bloody freezing. Did the temp drop a few degrees while we were in there?"

Will laughed. "You're such a wimp. Are all Aussies as delicate as you?"

"I'm not delicate. I just happen to have nerves in my skin, unlike you. Do they remove yours at birth over here?"

Beren shook his head. "Nope. We're just born tougher."

I rolled my eyes. "Oh, please. You guys strip down to your underwear in public when it's twenty-three degrees."

Liv laughed. "Okay, you have us there."

"Too right, I do." I looked Will up and down, wishing it was actually twenty-three degrees. He caught me and smirked. I grinned. After living together for the past few weeks, care of Angelica insisting he'd be safer under her roof, I was beyond the blushing stage. He knew how I felt, and I'd seen him in less than his underwear, finally. It had been well worth the wait, let me tell you. Anyway….

"Ooh, we have thirty minutes before Costa shuts. Let's grab a hot chocolate."

I shivered. "Liv, you're a genius. That sounds like a great idea."

It wasn't a long walk from the church to Costa, and because I was keen to get out of the cold, we did it in record time. I practically dragged Will the whole way, Liv and Beren almost jogging to keep up. Even though I was determined to get there quickly, I still took note of my surroundings. After Will, Angelica, and James almost got killed less than a month ago, I was not taking any chances, plus the snake group was still after me too. None of us could afford to be anything but vigilant.

As usual, it was a haven of warmth, divinely delicious smells, and animated chatter. We got our orders and managed to snag a table at a window. The reflections meant the view outside wasn't super clear, but the Christmas lights strung up on the buildings shone through. It was so pretty. The only thing that would have made it perfect would have been snow, but as cold as it was, snow was still rare around here. At least it wasn't as rare as in Cronulla, Sydney, where it was as likely as me passing on a cappuccino and chocolate muffin. If things weren't so dangerous, we could pop away to Switzerland. Now *that* would be awesome.

I cradled my hot chocolate between slowly thawing hands and breathed in the sweet hot-chocolate vapours. Mmm… chocolate.

"You enjoying yourself there?" Will smirked. "Sometimes I think you love coffee and chocolate more than me."

I looked at him. "And?" Liv and I laughed while Will feigned shock and despair.

"Oh," said Liv, regarding me shyly. This wasn't normal Liv behaviour. "I was wondering if you lot would like to come to my parents' for dinner on Friday night. Um, it's my birthday. But you don't have to if you don't want."

I sat up straight. "What?! Of course I'd love to come, and where I go, Will goes."

"Of course we'll be there, Livvy." Beren grabbed her hand and smiled. "There's nothing we wouldn't do for you, and besides, that sounds like fun."

She blushed. "Thanks. But only if you're sure."

I rolled my eyes. "What's gotten into you, Liv? We're your best friends. There's nothing that would stop us from going… as long as there's cake." I waggled my eyebrows. I vaguely remembered us telling each other when our birthdays were, but my memory was terrible. I'd put it in my phone to give me a reminder the day before so I wouldn't forget, but I probably should have set it for a week or two before, to make sure we organised in time to celebrate. Lucky her mum had it under control.

She laughed. "Of course there'll be cake. I don't know…. It's just that this is the first year I won't be spending it with my old friends, and, well, you know…. I just wanted to be sure we were good." By "you know," she meant her now-dead ex-fiancé who my brother, James, had killed to save me. She'd had so much upheaval through that. No wonder a bit of insecurity was creeping in.

I reached across the table and grabbed her other hand.

"We're besties, Liv. Don't ever forget that. I know we haven't known each other for years and years, but you're my people, and I'm yours."

She smiled. "Thanks."

Beren cleared his throat. "And I'm your man. Part of my duties include attending birthdays, Christmases, weddings of relatives you hate, christenings, looking after you when you're sick, and providing an unlimited supply of hugs and chocolate when you're sad." Liv gave him the most love-filled gaze. It was beyond sweet. I couldn't help smiling as my heart filled with gooey warmth. Rare moments when we were all happy had to be cherished. If it wasn't so creepy, I would have recorded the moment with my phone, although, with my luck, I'd see that someone was about to die.

Hmm, won't be doing that, then.

A woman's voice came from across the restaurant, near the cash register. "Oh, my goodness. Is that Roly-Poly?"

Olivia stiffened and put her hot chocolate down. She stared at me, eyes wide. It was as if she'd been caught doing something she shouldn't. My forehead tightened as I wrinkled it. The woman who'd called out was making her way over. She was about my age and height, super slim with huge boobs, and had really short, bleached-white hair. Her fake lashes reached our table about five minutes before she did. She stood at the end of the table where she could get a good look at Olivia. "It *is* you! How long has it been? Three years? Are you on your break? And look at you! You're not nearly as fat as you used to be."

What the hell? I couldn't work out if she was joking or

not. Surely someone wouldn't say those things to someone else and mean them. Except Liv's face told a different story. She glanced at Beren, panic streaking her face. She took a deep breath before turning to look at the short-haired woman. Beren met my gaze over the table. The tightness around his eyes meant he was just as unhappy as I was. If this woman was being cruel to the lady we loved, she'd better watch out because we weren't going to just let it go.

Liv put on her fake smile, the one that showed a little too much teeth. "Hi, Kate. I don't actually work here anymore, but I still like to visit. How have you been?"

"I've had cancer. Didn't your mum tell you?"

Liv shook her head. "Ah, no. Was she supposed to know?"

"Well, my mum ran into her a few months back. Anyway, I've been through two rounds of chemo, which finished a few weeks ago, and now I'm waiting for the all-clear. You know I'd never cut my hair to look like this." She rolled her eyes and pointed to her short do.

"Well, it looks great. Lucky short hair suits you." Full points to Olivia for being as nice as possible, but it was true —Kate would probably look good bald. How annoying.

Kate giggled. "I know, but thanks. So, are you going to introduce me to your friends?" Her lips slid into a sultry smile as she tilted her head and gazed at Beren, then Will. If I didn't hate her before, I sure hated her now. I looked at Liv and raised a brow. Instead of laughing, like she would have normally done, her eyes were wide—gah, she was still panicking. Did she think Beren and Will were that easily swayed?

I looked up at Kate and smiled. I was aiming for happy with a bit of shark mixed in for good measure. Her sexy smile faltered. Job. Done. "Hi, Kate. I'm Lily, and this is Will and Beren. Any friend of Olivia's is a friend of ours." She wasn't even looking at me—she was busy biting her lip while she gazed down at Beren. And was she actually batting her eyelashes? "And any enemy of Olivia's is an enemy of ours." I narrowed my eyes as she finally looked my way. She paused mid lip bite. "And anyone flirting with Olivia's boyfriend gets enemy status. I'm pretty sure Liv has nothing left to say to you. Congratulations on beating cancer. Goodbye." My heart pounded. I'd never been so rude to anyone who wasn't trying to kill me, and I couldn't help but think I was overreacting—maybe she hadn't been flirting, and I was making a huge fool of myself.

Her mouth dropped open. She closed it and opened it a couple of times like a suffocating fish. Her composure returned with narrowed eyes, which she levelled at Olivia. "I'd never be friends with someone as big as you anyway, and who wants a guy with a fat-woman fetish." She smirked at Beren, tossed her head—which lacked the desired effect, as her hair was too short—and walked away.

I breathed out, hating my heart for racing. I was so crap at confrontation. "Good riddance. I love it when the garbage takes itself out. Are you okay, Liv? She was horrible." I shook my head.

Olivia quickly wiped one eye. "I'll be okay." Her voice

was soft, meek. Wow, that evil woman must have really done a number on her.

Beren put his arm around her and pulled her into his side. "Where do you know her from?"

"School. Her and her group gave me a hard time, but I'm okay now. I did used to be fat, and I know I still need to lose some weight, but—"

"No, you don't!" Beren scowled. "You're perfect the way you are. You're an amazing woman, Liv, and I wouldn't change a thing about you." Beren caressed her cheek. "I never want to hear you put yourself down again. I love you, and I have impeccable taste." He winked.

"Ditto," I said. "Liv, that chick and her friends—what they did to you says more about them than you. I think you're awesome. You're gorgeous, stylish, and you're not fat at all. Even if you were, I wouldn't care. I wouldn't love you any less, and if I ever put on lots of weight, I expect your full support too." I grinned and looked at my almost-finished double-chocolate muffin. Yep, not giving those up. "Please just put all that out of your mind. High school's behind you now. If she ever says anything to you again, I'm going to put a fat spell on her—not because I think being fat is awful, but it's her worst nightmare. Let her get a dose of reality."

Liv's frown quirked up into a small smile. "I would never ask you to do that to someone, but in this case, I wouldn't dream of stopping you. You know, for educational purposes only."

I snorted. "Yep, *educational purposes*."

We finished our food, although I noticed Olivia left half her toasted sandwich on her plate. Beren, not even wondering why, checked if she was done with it, then ate it —typical man. Liv hardly ever left food on her plate. I was pretty sure I knew why she'd done it this time though. Hopefully, she'd forget all about that stupid girl in the next few days and go back to her normal self.

As we left Costa, I crossed my fingers—not exactly the best way to ensure things went how you wanted, but it was the best I had.

Outside it may have been freezing, but there were pretty lights, smiling faces, and the scent of Christmas in the air. We strode along the high street, then turned right towards Angelica's place. Beren's phone rang. "Hi, Auntie…. Mmm hmm. Yes…. Okay. We'll be there in five. Bye."

Will whispered the bubble-of-silence spell. "What is it, B?"

"Angelica needs us at a crime scene. A non-witch shot himself in his barn. There was a trace of magic at the scene, but the signature isn't on file. Kent police are handing it over to us. Angelica hasn't got anyone else available right now. She's also asked if you can attend, Lily, and take some photos."

"Oh, okay. Can I wait till everything is cleaned up and the body removed? I don't think I need to see… well, you know." I wasn't an agent, and all that gruesome stuff made my stomach turn and gave me nightmares. I was happy to help with my special talent, but I didn't want to have to see everything. There was a reason I hadn't taken up Angelica's offer to become an agent—well, that was one of a few reasons, but it was still an important one.

"I suppose so," said Beren. "I'll get Will to come get you when we're ready. It'll probably be sometime after midnight though. Are you okay with that?"

I shrugged. "Meh. I haven't got anything on tomorrow, so I can sleep in."

"Okay, great."

We reached home, and as soon as we went inside, Will kissed me goodbye; then he and Beren left. Liv and I watched some TV before she went to bed, and I waited up. It was going to be a long night.

CHAPTER 2

The next day, I woke to an empty bed at eleven. Will had finally taken me to the crime scene at one in the morning. He'd had to wake me after I'd fallen asleep on the couch watching *The Day of the Triffids*. Probably not a great movie choice late at night. After I returned from work, I had nightmares of plants trying to eat me during some weird, green-tinged twilight. Yeah, nah. Not my smartest decision. Will had come home with me at 2:00 a.m., but now he was gone, probably back at work. The PIB had a punishing work schedule.

After dressing, I wandered downstairs. It was late to be having my first cup of coffee. If I didn't imbibe some of the good stuff soon, I'd get a migraine. I found Liv in the kitchen, her hand resting on the lid of the blender, which was whizzing almost loud enough to shake the house. I put my hands over my ears and yelled, "Good morning."

Liv turned and smiled. She switched the blender off. "Good morning!"

I lowered my hands and magicked a cappuccino into existence. I wasn't exactly sure how it happened, but I knew my magic collated all the ingredients from my kitchen and, voila: one hot, gorgeously fragrant coffee sat in my hands. "What are you making?" I asked as I sat at the table.

"Fruit smoothie, with strawberry, banana, melon, blueberries, and low-fat milk." She poured it into a large cup and sat next to me.

"Hmm, looks… healthy." I eyed it while sipping my coffee. Banana and milk were okay, but melon and milk? I did my best not to pull a face.

"Why are you making a funny face."

Whoops, failed. I really should take Angelica's poker-face class. "Don't mind me. I just woke up. You know I'm useless until I've at least finished one cup of coffee."

"How did last night go?"

"I got nothing, which is to say, the guy killed himself without any help. They can't work out when or why magic was lingering, but there's nothing to say it had anything to do with what happened. Neutral, Angelica called it, whatever that means."

"Ah." She nodded. "I think they can tell if it had bad intentions, so if it was magic created to hurt someone."

"How come you know, and I don't?" It wasn't the first time Angelica had failed to explain something important. "I've never heard it mentioned."

She shrugged and sipped her smoothie, her face carefully blank. Ha! I'd bet she thought it tasted yuck, and she was pretending it was okay. But after last night, I wasn't going to make her feel bad. She was obviously on a health kick. Hopefully it wouldn't last too long—I needed someone to be decadent with me at Costa. It was never as much fun being the only person eating the unhealthy stuff. It was a bonding experience, eating cake with your bestie, something that's been a thing for generations, or at least the last thirty years, surely. My mum used to have high tea with her friends. She did that at least a couple of times a year. After all, celebrations were only a "celeb" unless you also had the "rations": it might look good, but you were going to leave hungry. Not my idea of fun times.

"You probably never needed to know. Every time they've found magic signatures, it meant a crime was committed, so they probably didn't bother saying there was even something else to look out for."

I shrugged. Whatever. There was always so much to learn, but since I wasn't in law enforcement, I didn't need to know. I'd let the PIB figure that stuff out. I had enough problems. Liv's phone rang. She answered it. "Hello, Ma'am. Yes?" After a moment, she handed the phone to me. "It's for you."

"Oh, okay." I took it. "Hello?"

"Hello, dear. Where's your phone?"

"Upstairs in my room."

"Try to remember to keep it with you. I could contact you mind to mind, but it takes a ridiculous amount of energy, and it might surprise you at the wrong moment. I could just see you falling down the stairs and breaking your neck." She laughed. I opened my eyes wide. What the hell? "Anyway, enough of the jokes. We need your services again. I'm going to send you some coordinates. And don't worry; there isn't anything gory. You'll be landing in one of our vans, which is in the car park of the Sevenoaks Community Centre. You'll be going inside to a dance recital competition thing. Anyway, dear, stand by for the coordinates. Will is there. He'll explain what you're looking for."

Large golden numbers appeared in my mind. I magicked my coffee cup clean and away. "Gotta go, Liv. I'll be back later. Are you going to be around?"

"Yep, except I'm going to the gym. If I'm not here, that's where I am. Stay safe, Lil."

I smiled and magicked my camera to my hand. "I will. Bye." I made my doorway, imprinted the coordinates on the front, then stepped through. On the other side, I pushed the black curtain out of the way, revealing a van fitted out in a similar fashion to the one we'd worked from on the nursing-home case. I shuddered. Beren and Ma'am had both pretty much died on that assignment. Will's gran had died. I shook my head quickly, dispelling the downward slide of my thoughts before it began. I was here to help solve a case.

The van door slid open, and my favourite person stuck his head in. He smiled, showing off his adorable dimples. "It's my favourite woman."

I checked my mind shield—it was up. "You stole my thought. I was just thinking you were my favourite person." I smiled.

He gave me a quick hug and kiss on the lips. "Thanks for coming."

"I do what I can. It's not easy being this awesome."

He snorted. "Yes, well, Miss Awesome, I need you to take a few photos. See if anyone cast any spells here in the last few weeks."

"What happened? Is it horrible?"

"It's not nice, but I wouldn't say horrible, at least, not in the way you mean. There was a dancing competition. Participants were from five to eleven years old—they ran age categories for tap, ballet, and modern dance. During the competition for the eight-year-olds, one girl was coming fourth, and the three girls who normally beat her all mysteriously injured themselves during their performances. One girl broke her foot, the other sprained her ankle, and the last one broke her arm when she slipped and fell. Imani happened to be here watching her niece dance and picked up on the faint feel of magic just before each of the girls was injured."

"Well, that's weird. And she couldn't see if there were any witches in the audience?"

"There were two, but we've questioned them and let them go—the magic signatures don't match. Come on. I'll show you where it happened."

I hopped out of the van and surveyed the car park. I might as well see if the person had been out here when the injuries happened. I turned my Nikon on and held it up. "Show me anyone who has performed magic here today." Nothing changed. The same five cars sat in the same spots.

No people popped out of nowhere. I lowered the camera and shook my head. Will shrugged and started towards the community centre—a single-storey brick building that was built in the 1970s, by the looks of things. Nothing exciting—just a boring but functional municipal building.

Inside, the large hall was filled with rows of plastic chairs, all facing a stage. Glitter and bits and pieces of rubbish littered the floor. I shook my head. Two garbage bins sat next to the entry—why couldn't people just use them?

Imani stood on the stage with two agents, but other than that, there was only one other woman. She stood in front of the stage, looking up nervously. One hand was at her neck, rolling a pearl-looking necklace between her fingers. I used my other-sight to determine she was a non-witch. What excuse had the agents given her for their presence?

I raised my camera. "Show me someone using magic here in the last two weeks." Light disappeared. The rows of chairs remained, but now they contained dark figures watching the stage, which was lit by spotlights. A child, maybe ten or eleven years old, sat at a baby grand piano. The child was dressed in a tuxedo—how cute. I snapped a couple of photos, but my attention was drawn to the front row, where a faint golden glow surrounded someone.

I carefully walked down the middle aisle between the chairs, not wanting to lower my camera in case I lost the image. The woman in the front row had dark straight hair, gently curled and falling to her shoulders. She wore a sly smile, and a baby-pink coat over dark pants. I snapped a few shots, then turned and snapped shots of the child on the stage.

"Hey, Lily."

Damn. I lowered the camera and looked up at Imani. She was standing by herself—the two agents had disappeared, although they probably walked off, as that woman was standing there, and we didn't want any heart attacks. "Hey. How's it going?" I smiled. I was happy to see her, but I hated being disturbed when I was in the middle of things.

"Good, love." She walked down the stairs and stood next to me. "Can I have a look?"

"Yeah, sure." I handed her the camera. I would've liked to have taken a closer shot of the boy on the stage to see if there were any similarities between him and the woman performing magic. At this stage, I had no idea if the magic was to help or hinder him. Maybe she'd flung him off his piano stool trying to break his wrist? "What do you think's going on there?"

"I don't remember seeing her here today, and this would've been from another night. They have things here all the time. Hang on." She handed my camera back and approached the woman who was worriedly looking on. While Imani spoke to the lady, I got up on stage and stood near where the boy had been. "Show me the boy playing piano." Phew, he was still there. I focussed on his face and clicked. The emotion on his face as his fingers pressed the keys made it obvious he was enjoying himself and totally into the piece.

I turned back and snapped one more shot of the

woman. Maybe she'd been trying to make him play better? Now that I'd seen both of them close up, there was a resemblance. Was that his mother?

Raising the camera one more time, I said, "Show me the last person to perform magic here." The same woman sat there, faintly glowing. Right. I turned the camera off and joined Imani in front of the stage. The other lady had started sweeping the mess up.

Imani said, "Let's go outside. We're done here. We'll join Will in the van and discuss our findings."

I followed her outside to the van. Once we were sitting inside with the door closed, Will asked. "What do you have for me?"

"Here." I handed him the camera. "Not much, at least not from today."

As he flicked through the photos, Imani said, "That's from a week ago. There was a school music night. Nothing happened, and, in fact, that boy's performance went off splendidly, so if anything, she was probably helping him."

I rolled my eyes. Some parents would do anything to make their kids seem perfect. And did the kid realise what his mum had done? Unless she could be with him all the time to make everything he did look good, he would learn the hard way one day that he wasn't as awesome as he thought. That was going to be a hell of a difficult day for that kid.

"So all we've got from today are three injured kids and a magic signature?" I asked.

"Looks like it." Imani pursed her lips. "There was definitely no one doing the magic while we were there, unless they'd done it from outside."

"Nope. I checked when I got here. The only person to perform magic here in the last week was that woman at the music night."

Imani folded her arms and blew an errant dark curl off her forehead. "I hate unanswered questions. Well, I guess there's nothing else we can do right now. One of the kids that got hurt is my niece's friend. I'll call my sister shortly and see if she can find anything else out with some subtle questioning."

"Was your sister one of the other two witches here today?" I asked.

"No. She had to work. I was the family representative. I'm an awesome aunt." She grinned.

"You definitely are, but where's your niece now?" I wasn't sure if she'd noticed, but there were no kids around.

She laughed. "She had a friend's birthday party after this, so that friend's mother picked her up on the way through."

"Ah, cool. I was a bit worried about your auntieing skills for a minute there." Also, that kid had a much better social life than I did. Sad, really. I remember wanting to reach eighteen so I could go out whenever and to wherever I wanted, but at twenty-four, I was lucky if I went out clubbing once every six months. When did I get so *old?* Hmm, now I remember. It was when I came to England. A pang booped me in the chest—I missed my Sydney friends. It had been at least a month since I'd contacted any of them. I was a slack friend, but they were probably busy and hardly knew I was gone anymore. I sighed.

"Are you okay, Lily?" Will stared at me, a little divot between his brows.

"Sorry, just thinking. So, what now?"

"Well, I've got to get back to headquarters and write up the report on today. Imani, you're not actually supposed to be working, so you can get on with your day."

I turned to her. "Why don't you come hang out with me and Liv. Maybe we'll go into London or something."

She shrugged. "Sounds good to me."

We bade Will goodbye—me with a kiss, Imani with a wave. The afternoon was shaping up to be a pleasant one, but I couldn't help thinking there was more to this than any of us thought. And I didn't want to brag, but I was right more often than not, especially when I didn't want to be. Thanks, Universe, thanks a lot.

CHAPTER 3

Will, Imani, Liv and I stood on Liv's parents' front porch. This was the second time I'd been back since Liv's engagement—the day Will had almost died trying to read her fiancé's mind. Hmm, my friends and I did a lot more almost-dying than the average group of people. The two-storey character home was just as grand as I remembered it, albeit it was dark now, and I couldn't see as clearly as last time.

Liv paused before putting her key in the lock. "What's wrong, birthday girl?" I asked.

She looked at me. "I don't know. I've just got a weird feeling. It's not usually this quiet. Normally Oscar is barking at the door by now and Mum has hurried to come answer it. She always gets there before I manage to get it open."

I shrugged. "She's probably just getting dinner organised. Come on. It's too cold to stand out here." I smiled.

"Aren't we going to wait for B?" She frowned. Ah, that's what she was worried about. I gently elbowed Will. He didn't notice. I rolled my eyes, then elbowed him harder.

"Oh, oh, yes. He's just had a big day at work. Angelica had him attending a crime scene at four. He'll be here soon. Don't worry."

Liv looked at her phone. "It's already six thirty. What if he doesn't make dinner?"

Imani put a hand on her shoulder. "Don't worry, love. He'll be here, and I bet he makes it up to you." She waggled her eyebrows, and I laughed.

Liv blushed, and a small smile curled her lips up. "I suppose you're right." She turned and slid the key into the lock. A burst of warm air flowed over us as we walked in. Will was the last in, and he shut the door behind himself. Our steps echoed on the floorboards as we walked through the vestibule into the main living area, Olivia leading the way.

I sniffed the air. "Mmm, is that garlic bread I smell?"

"Surprise!" a chorus of voices rang out. People jumped up from behind furniture, and a muffled dog's bark came from the back garden.

My hand shot to my chest. Liv stood in shock. My brain's go-to was to make a joke, especially when it wasn't appropriate. "Wow, all this just because there's garlic bread?" It was Will's turn to elbow me. He had no sense of humour. "What? I was just making a joke."

Liv's mother, her slim frame dressed elegantly in an emerald-green, long-sleeve wrap dress, glided over and took her daughter's arm. Her mother smiled and gave her a kiss on the cheek. "Happy birthday, Liv, darling."

Her father walked up and put his arm around her. "We know you didn't want anything huge, but we wanted to surprise you. You've had a rough year, and, well, we wanted you to know how many people care about you. Happy birthday." He kissed her forehead. Liv gave them a smile, but it looked like her tentative one—the one that meant she wasn't sure whether she wanted to smile or not.

As her mother handed her a small box wrapped in pink paper with a silver bow around it, a few of those who'd yelled "surprise" gathered around her, pushing Will, Imani, and I back. And one of those people was Kate, the vile woman from the other night.

Just great.

Will and I shared a worried glance. And why was Kate here after we insulted her? Surely she knew she wasn't welcome. There was no sign of that when she leaned in to give Liv a hug. My friend pasted on her fake smile. In Kate's spiderlike embrace, the worry in Liv's eyes turned to despair. Liv turned her head slightly to look at me. That was my cue. I pushed through the crowd and grabbed her arm. "Liv hasn't felt well today. Can everyone just give her some breathing room?" I was the queen of making things up on the fly, especially in desperate times.

Thankfully, I didn't have to pull out my magic to get everyone to comply. Kate dropped her arms, and everyone moved back. A couple of people said, "I'm sorry. Oh no, are you okay?" At least they weren't all horrible like Kate, at least I didn't think so. But then, for all I knew, they'd all been part of the group at school who'd made life hell for her.

Liv's mum, stripes of worry lining her forehead, took her daughter's hand. "I didn't know you weren't feeling well. Come and sit down." As she led Liv and I towards the back of the house, she called over her shoulder. "Come on through, everyone, and let's have some refreshments."

The living area that led to the back garden had been transformed from its usual elegance. Fake bats hung from the ceiling, as did silver stars on strings, and spiders. Waiters stood around, holding either trays of full wine and champagne glasses or hors d'oeuvres. Katy Perry's latest song played at a comfortable volume through inset ceiling speakers.

Liv's mum settled us on the couch. "Are you okay? Would you like me to call this off, send everyone home?" Gee, her mum was nice. This must have cost a fortune, but she was putting her daughter first.

Liv smiled. "I'll be okay. I think it was just the shock of seeing… everyone." By everyone, I knew she meant Kate, but there were others she could be talking about too. And, in fact, there was one couple I recognised from her engagement party, but I remembered them being quite nice. Anyway, once her mum was gone, I'd get the lowdown.

"I agree. Even I was surprised," I added. "I'll make sure she's okay, Mrs Grosvenor."

"How many times have I told you to call me Cassandra,

Lily." She shook her head. "Okay, I'll entrust Liv into your care. If you need anything, let me know."

I smiled up at her, and Liv said, "We will. Thanks, Mum. And thank you for going to all this effort. The place looks amazing."

"Well, I know how much you love all that mysterious stuff, like fortune telling. I actually have someone coming." She looked at her watch. "They should be here in twenty minutes. Guess who it is?" Her face brightened with barely contained glee.

Liv's mouth dropped open. "Oh my God! You didn't?!"

Her mother grinned. "I did."

Liv jerked her head around to look at me, excitement replacing the haunted look in her eyes. "Owen the Oracle is coming. He's the best fortune teller ever. He's famous, but he does special events, and even though he travels Europe doing shows, he's from Westerham." She turned back to her mother. "But isn't he ridiculously expensive?"

She shrugged. "Don't worry yourself, darling. We can afford it, and we love to make you happy. Enjoy your night. We love you." She bent down and gave her a hug, then straightened. "Now, I have things to do. If you need anything, let me know."

"Ooh, I've heard he's good." Imani nodded.

"Do you believe in that stuff?" I asked. First ghosts, and now fortune tellers. For some reason, I didn't think witches were into things like that. I mean, having power meant they could see that stuff was fake, didn't it?

"Not really, but my mother does." She lowered her

voice. "She has a small talent for reading tea leaves. She uses her you-know-what to help, of course." She winked. Right, so it wasn't necessarily a real thing that just happened—it took magic to make it work, and even then, I doubted it was super accurate about everything. That would make life way too easy.

Two waiters came over, one with the drinks tray, the other with the food one. We each grabbed a glass of champers and tiny pancakes with smoked salmon topped with crème cheese and dill. I popped it into my mouth. Mmm, so good. I chased it with a sip of champagne. "Are you going to open your mum's gift?" I'd given her a present earlier that day: a gift voucher to a gourmet tea shop. She seemed to have recovered from the tea-and-violence debacle from a few months ago, and, thankfully, she'd liked the present.

"It's wrapped so beautifully. I hate ruining the paper."

"Sacrifices must be made. Go on."

Imani nodded.

Liv grinned. "If you both insist." She undid the bow and carefully picked the sticky tape off the wrapping. It was taking too long, and it was all I could do not to lean over and grab it out of her hands. *Patience, Lily.* Finally, a little blue velvet box was revealed. She opened it, unveiling a pair of silver-coloured dove earrings. The birds were in flight, small diamonds trailing down their wings. Knowing her parents, the earrings weren't silver but white gold or platinum, but it didn't matter. What mattered was, they were stunning. "They're gorgeous. Put them on!"

She smiled. "These have another meaning too. I was,

obviously, born close to Christmas, and Mum had trouble conceiving, so they always called me their Christmas miracle." She took out the hoop earrings she'd been wearing and put them in her clutch, then put the doves in.

Imani stared at them. "They're so pretty!"

"Gorgeous," I agreed. I took my phone out of my bag, cut my magic off so I wouldn't get any nasty surprises—which I hated because it always left me feeling bereft—then took her photo. Then Imani, Liv, and I jammed together, and I took a selfie. Done, I put my phone back in my bag and let my magic in again.

"It was off to a rocky start, but this is turning into a good birthday," Liv said. "I can't wait to see Owen. I've had my fortune read a couple of times, but it's very hit-and-miss. He's supposed to be amazingly accurate."

I'd asked Imani before. Now it was Liv's turn to get the interrogation. "Do you really believe in the future-telling stuff?"

"Kind of. I mean, I know most of them are fake, but my auntie went to see him a couple of years ago, just before he got famous, and everything he said came true."

"Like what?"

"He said she was going to get the job she wanted—which she didn't even tell him about. And she got it, about three weeks later. He also told her that my cousin, her daughter, would get the marks she wanted to get into university, and she did."

"But that could have happened anyway." I didn't think

that was definitive proof this guy could read peoples' futures.

"He also said they'd get a new dog, a poodle, within the next two months, and they did."

I still wasn't convinced. "But maybe they did because he put the idea into her mind?"

She shook her head. "Nope. The dog they had at the time was a poodle, and he couldn't have known, and it died. My auntie and her husband went and got another one."

"Hmm, well, I guess that could be more than a coincidence." I still wasn't totally convinced, but I had to concede the coincidences were adding up. The waiter lowered his tray of smoked-salmon goodies in front of me. I took another one. They were too good to pass up. "These are delish."

"They're my favourite." Liv took another one and popped it into her mouth.

"Hey, Liv. Are you feeling better now?" A familiar-looking slim girl with long, straight blonde hair stood in front of where Liv sat.

"Yes. It was just the surprise." She smiled. "Ellen, this is Lily and Imani. Lily and Imani, this is Ellen. We worked at Costa together." Ah, so she's probably a nice person, and no wonder I recognised her.

"Lovely to meet you, Ellen. I love Costa's coffee and chocolate muffins. I haven't seen you there lately, though." I felt bad for not really recognising her.

She replied, "I stopped working there just before Liv left. I finally managed to get a job in finance in London. I have a degree, but it's taken me a year and a half to find a job."

"Yikes. That's tough. But congratulations." I smiled.

"Thanks. So, Liv, how's your new job?"

As they chatted, I sipped my drink and let my gaze wander the room. There were about twenty guests. And guess who was fawning all over my boyfriend? My stomach dropped. Will had reassured me that he had hardly any dealings with Piranha while he'd been undercover and then trapped, but he generally didn't want to talk about it, and I believed him… 95 percent. Let's face it—I'd be naïve to trust someone else 100 percent; I didn't even trust myself the whole time. I'd done things I hadn't intended to do and disappointed myself on occasion, and no one was perfect. Seeing another woman running her hand down his arm and giggling didn't inspire confidence. At least he was scowling. And it seemed as if she needed backup in the form of a tall, leggy brunette. Her friend was laughing at something Kate had just said. I rolled my eyes. Give me a break.

Will caught my gaze and raised a brow, giving me a "come save me" look. I was in half a mind to leave him to his fate, considering he was old enough to excuse himself, especially after what happened the other night. Wasn't he even worried about hurting Olivia's feelings by cosying up to her sworn enemy? I stood, but I wasn't doing this for me; I was doing this for Olivia. I hated being a jealous girlfriend, but the last few months had pushed me as far as I could go, and at this point, Will's and my relationship had had more downs than ups.

As I reached them, Will said, "There's my gorgeous girl." He grabbed my hand and pulled me close. I slammed into his side. Kate scowled but quickly masked it with a smile. Her friend raised a brow and gave Kate a "this chick isn't any competition" look. Well, leggy friend, just watch it. I narrowed my eyes at both of them.

At the risk of sound like a psychotically jealous girlfriend, and probably revealing my insecurity, which wasn't a great idea, I said, "So, *Kate*, I guess you don't think I'm fat."

She looked at me with scrunched eyes and furrowed forehead. "What?"

"Didn't you say you don't go for guys who have, and I quote, 'a fat-woman fetish?'" I wanted to fold my arms, but Will was gripping my hand so hard that there was no way it would make its destination. He was probably telling me to tone it down, but forget it, buster. If no one else was going to call a spade a spade, or, in this case, a homewrecker a homewrecker, I'd have to. "Stop flirting with my boyfriend." I leaned closer to her. "And, if you do anything to upset Olivia tonight, I'll make sure you regret it. Understood?" I glared so hard that my eyeballs ached. I hadn't even known that was possible.

Her friend snarled. "Don't you dare threaten my best friend. You'd better watch it, Skippy." I felt a flare of magic and used my other sight. She was a witch. Did Kate know about witches, or was she oblivious to her friend's *specialness*? And seriously, Skippy? That wasn't even offensive. I'd be happy to be a kangaroo any day; I'd prefer to be a squirrel, but, hey, bouncing around all day had merit.

Kate pressed her lips together, and her nostrils flared as she took in an angry breath. "I'll do what I like, and no convict is going to tell me what to do." She gave me a dirty look, then smiled at Will, a seductive gleam in her eyes. "We can chat again later." Her friend smirked as if it were a done deal.

"Actually, no we can't. The woman I love feels uncomfortable with me talking to you, so I'm going to pass, but I hope you have a lovely night." Will looked at me and smiled while Kate and her witchy friend stalked off. Will's smile crept into a frown. He whispered, "Maybe tone it down a tad? We're supposed to be having fun at a party. And a little trust would be nice."

I looked up at him and kept my voice low. Unfortunately, my anger had fizzled away, and now I just felt like an overreactive idiot. "She was flirting with you, and she hurt Olivia's feelings. She's evil, and you just stand here chatting with her like she's the most interesting thing ever. Where's your loyalty to Olivia?" *Or me.* But yes, I was too gutless to say it. Who knew, maybe he thought my behaviour was crazy, and he'd break up with me later.

He whispered in my ear, sending goosebumps down my neck. "I love you, and no one can ever come between us." He kissed my cheek. "And I was trying to be polite and not create a scene. Goodness knows Olivia's had enough shocks for one night. I always have your back and hers. You need to trust me, Lil. But it's nice that you care so much." He winked.

I sighed. If I didn't learn to trust him, we weren't going to last very long. "I'm sorry. It didn't look good, though."

"What do you mean? Was my 'please save me' face not enough?"

"You could've left the conversation without causing a scene."

"Ha! I tried. I even said, I'm going to go sit with Lily now, and she grabbed my arm, did her stupid giggle, and begged me not to leave. She said she didn't know many people here."

"Why are you men so gullible when it comes to women?"

"Don't worry. I'm not gullible; I'm being careful not to cause a scene. Do you know why Olivia's mother thought it was okay to invite someone who's given her so much grief?"

"I haven't had a chance to ask Liv yet. She probably thinks they're friends. I'm assuming Liv didn't tell her mother any of what happened at school, or the other day." I narrowed my eyes. Yes, I'd been keeping tabs on the spikey blonde after she'd walked away; never turn your back on danger. Her eyes lit up as she looked past her friends to the door. Beren had arrived. "She's got her sights on B. Can you grab him and bring him over to Liv?"

"Aye, aye, captain." He gave my hand a gentle squeeze and hurried over to Beren. I returned to Liv, who was talking to Ellen and another guy. Imani had wandered off to chat to a couple of others.

I sat at the end of the sofa while Liv made introductions; then Will and Beren joined us. We chatted amiably until the night's entertainment arrived in a flourish of black cape and red beret. Interesting combo. He looked more like an eccentric artist than a fortune teller. His moustache and beard reminded me of Edward Norton in *The Illusionist*.

Two guys in black turtleneck jumpers and tight black jeans followed him in and set up a table in one corner of the room. Owen the Oracle stood in the centre of the room and called out above the noise while his posse erected a black tall tent thing around the table. Looked like whatever happened in Owen's oracle tent stayed in Owen's oracle tent. I snorted. The man himself spoke. "Good evening, ladies and gentlemen. I am Owen the Oracle, famous and accurate predictor of the future." He set his gaze upon the birthday girl and swept his arm up with all the drama of an actor giving the Shakespearean performance of his life. He held his hand out towards Liv. "I would like to invite the birthday girl to be the first to have her fortune read. Please join me in my sanctuary."

Well, that was creepy. Was it a sanctuary or a lair? And how much were they paying for these theatrics? Maybe this was what they enjoyed? All the guests stared at him in awe. Maybe he *was* good. After Liv disappeared inside his tent and everyone went back to chatting, I turned to Will and Beren and used my inside voice. "Do you think he's legit?"

My scalp prickled with someone else's magic. It wasn't the normal severe, "I want to scratch my head itch," but it was there, nevertheless. What the hell? I flicked my gaze around the room.

"It's okay, Lily," said Will. "That oracle guy's a witch.

He probably uses magic to make himself seem more mysterious."

"Hmm, maybe. Could he be putting a spell on them so they answer questions to all their deepest, darkest secrets? Then he knows what to say to them before making them forget he ever asked."

"That would use way too much power, and if he had those kinds of incredible skills, he'd be one of only a handful of witches. It's possible, but extremely unlikely. Don't worry, Lily. It's probably just to make his act better. Besides, if he has that skill, he'll pick up on a few random thoughts from his subjects because they can't make mind-shields." Will put his arm around me and pulled me close.

"Oh no. Maybe I should have shielded Liv's mind before she went in. Did you think of that, Beren?"

He shook his head and shrugged. "She'll be okay, plus she'll think it's good when he can tell her some of the things she's worried about will be fine."

I was glad he was okay with it, but that was lying. The guy might know what she was worried about—I mean, I knew she was worried about Beren liking her, her weight thanks to stupid Kate—but how could he accurately predict how those things would play out? Even I couldn't guarantee things would go how she wanted. No one could.

Will kissed my forehead. "Don't worry, Lily. Enjoy Liv's birthday. It's all a bit of fun."

Was I being a stick in the mud? I supposed I was. Right. Time to enjoy myself and stop worrying. There was always so much to stress about, and I was probably just in the habit of thinking the worst. "I have been overthinking things lately. Sorry."

Will quirked his mouth up on one side in a half smile. "Hey, you care. There's nothing wrong with that. But there's a time to worry, and a time to enjoy yourself. Tonight is definitely the latter."

I flagged the waiter over and grabbed another drink. If I was going to have fun, I was going to do it properly. After twenty minutes, Olivia emerged from the tent, her expression bemused. As she reached us, Kate went into the tent. Wow, I wondered what thoughts he'd pick up from her. He'd better be careful, or he'd be traumatised.

Olivia had a definite spring in her step when she reached us. I grinned. "I take it the reading went well."

She nodded, her eyes wide. "Yes. And he was spot on with everything. It was unbelievable. No wonder he charges the big bucks."

I didn't think it was rude to ask since she brought it up, but even it was, I needed to know. "How expensive is he, exactly?"

"For parties, somewhere between ten and fifteen thousand quid."

My mouth dropped open. I was about to ask Will why all witches didn't just do this for a living, but then I realised it would burst Liv's bubble, so I, believe it or not, kept my mouth shut. Maybe that could be considered a Christmas miracle. "Um, wow."

"And in the interests of making the most of it, I expect you guys will all get your fortunes read too." Liv grinned.

I didn't believe in it, and I knew the guy couldn't read our minds, so it would probably be a bust, but tonight was about making Liv happy. "You know I'm a huge sceptic, but I'll give it a go." An Ed Sheeran song came on. "Let's dance, Liv. This is a celebration of your awesomeness, after all."

She grinned and took Beren's hand. I stood, grabbed Will, and we all made our way into the middle of the room. Once we were there having fun, a few more partygoers joined us. Eventually, Liv pushed me towards the oracle's booth. Owen's guys stood on either side of the entry flap. I took a breath. One of the men opened the flap for me, and I went in. *Do not roll your eyes. Do not make faces.*

It was warm in the confined space, and a hint of cinnamon and rosemary laced the air. I preferred the garlic-bread fragrance from when we arrived, but you couldn't have everything. Saliva exploded in my mouth. I was going to grab some of that garlic bread when I left, and I'd get Will to eat some too, so he wouldn't realise how bad my breath was later.

"Hello? Would you like to sit?" Oops, daydreaming strikes again. Owen the Oracle looked up at me, an intense look in his dark eyes. Telling fortunes was obviously his passion, or he was just creepy, and no one picked up on it because they expected their fortune teller to be weird.

I sat, my knees pushing against the requisite black fabric that draped over the table to the floor. An actual crystal ball hovered above the table, milky swirls shifting within its cold confines. Maybe that's what he used his magic for? Nice touch that wasn't too freaky. His clients might assume he had some kind of magician's trick going on to make it look like it was floating. I had to say, the cliché factor was high. If I was going to pretend to tell the future, I'd go understated. I clearly wasn't dramatic enough, so I'd probably fail if I tried. Best to stick to being able to see the past through my camera.

"Hi," I said.

He didn't smile—probably part of the act. "Welcome. Let's start with your name."

"I'm Lily."

"Lovely to meet you, Lily. Is there any specific area of your life you'd like me to look at?"

If he was so good, why did he need to ask? Obviously, if there was something I wanted to know, it was because things weren't going well. Massive clue for him. Oh well, why not put him to the test? My mind-shield was up, so he wasn't getting anything from me. If he got anything right, it was either because he had a special talent, or he was a good guesser.

"I'd like to know about my current romantic relationship. Will it last?"

"Okay. Please put your hands on the crystal ball."

"I thought that was your job. You're making me do all the work." I laughed because I was joking… kind of.

He looked at me, nothing but serious written across his face. Where was his sense of humour? "Once your hands are on the ball, I'll place mine on yours. Have no fear: Owen the Oracle wouldn't dream of slacking." Not another person who spoke about themselves in the third person. Didn't he know that was the domain of royalty?

I rested my palms on the cool glass, or was it really crystal, surface. "Is this glass or really crystal?" What? It was a legitimate question.

He blinked, and his top lip twitched, probably in annoyance. "It's crystal."

"Nice to know. Thanks." My enthusiasm was waning. He was taking all the fun out of this with his "I'm an important and mysterious fortune teller" demeanour.

Once my hands had settled, he placed his warm, damp hands on top of mine and shut his eyes. I pulled a face that I'm pretty sure distinctly conveyed the "ew" factor of the situation. Sweaty stranger's palms. Gross. He'd better have some good stuff to tell me. And to think, Liv's parents had paid thousands for this. I was sure I could think of much more entertaining ways to spend that. Think of all the trips to Costa that would buy, or how many romantic five-star-hotel stays. Yep, that would be way better than sitting in a tent with a guy who spoke of himself in the third person and had damp palms. I shuddered.

"It's okay, Lily. Many ladies are excited by being so close to Owen the Oracle—you're not the first, and you won't be the last. But don't worry; I would never take advantage."

My mouth dropped open. His eyes were still shut. Should I say something in my defence? I mean, I didn't want him thinking I liked him, but then what would I say? Sorry, you creep me out? I bit my tongue and swallowed my pride. I'd endure the awkwardness for my best friend's sake.

A gentle tingle caressed the back of my neck. It was for such a brief moment that I couldn't be sure whether it was magic or just me reacting to the situation. The milky swirls within the ball took on a hue like a fiery sunset, then coalesced into a picture of something, which I couldn't see clearly since my hands were covering half of it. I leaned to the side for a better look. My eyes widened. That looked a lot like Will in the clothes he was wearing tonight, at least the body did, and yep, that body close to him was Kate. What was that supposed to mean?

"Ah, now I see," Owen's voice was low and provocatively *knowing*. I hated when people did that. *Just get off your high horse and tell me already*. I so wanted to ask, but I kept my mouth shut. The picture confined in crystal morphed again. Will and I holding hands, a ghostly image standing behind us. I peered closer and wrinkled my forehead. That looked suspiciously like Kate. But what did it mean? "Yes, yes. Oh, yes." Owen's breathy outburst had me imagining what he would sound like during sex, and now the awkward factor just went up by one thousand. Why did my stupid brain have to go there?

I couldn't help it; my hands had a mind of their own. I pulled them away and wiped them on my jeans. "Sorry. My hands were itchy." If he couldn't tell me anything after all that, bad luck. I loved Liv, but there was only so much ickiness I could take.

He opened his eyes and smiled, showing too much teeth. "No matter. I have some interesting things to impart." He paused, probably for dramatic effect. I glanced at the tent door and sighed. So close, yet so far. He cleared his throat, so I looked back at him. "So, there is a woman you're worried about. I'm happy to tell you that although it may seem rocky at the moment, your boyfriend cares for you, and that other woman will soon be just a painful memory. You needn't worry yourself, Lily. I see you and your boyfriend going from strength to strength." Another tingle hit my nape, making my tiny hairs jump upright. I shivered. Owen's eyes narrowed just a fraction, but it was enough to clue me in that he knew something was going on with me. He would know I was a witch, but maybe he didn't expect me to pick up on the little bursts of power, if that's what they were.

"Is there anything else you can tell me?"

"No, Lily. That's it. I'd give you more of my time, but others are waiting. Thank you for stopping by to see me. I look forward to seeing you again one day." He smiled, and his chin tipped up. A dismissal?

"Thanks, Owen. It's been… interesting." I stood and left, eager to find out what he'd told Liv. As I made my way over, it was clear she was glaring at someone. I turned to see that someone glaring back at her. I'm sure you don't need two guesses. Yep, Kate. I hurried the rest of the way and stood in front of Liv, blocking her eye line to her least favourite person. "Hey. What's up?" Before she could answer, Beren arrived next to me holding one wine glass and one cocktail glass.

"Here you go, birthday girl." He handed her the cocktail.

"How was your fortune-telling session," Will asked, sliding his hands around my waist from behind.

I leaned into him. "Um, interesting, but not too interesting. No news to report. I'm keen to hear how Liv's went." I grinned at my friend.

She grinned back. "Mine was interesting too. But I'm not going to talk about it, just in case it's like when you make a wish—if you tell anyone, it won't come true."

"I don't think that applies here." I wasn't going to let her off that easily.

"Okay." She smirked. "I'll tell you mine if you tell me yours."

Hmm, I would tell her because it wasn't that secret, but not in front of Will and Beren. My insecurities were embarrassing, plus asking about a relationship was the safest option. I was pretty sure Will and I were fine and would continue to be, and if we weren't, well, there was nothing I could do about it. If being myself wasn't good enough, he didn't deserve me, but I happened to know he did like me, craziness and coffee addiction included. He was a keeper.

"You've got me there. Maybe we can chat about it later." I waggled my brows.

"Sounds good." She laughed.

Beren turned to Will. "Why do we miss out on the good stuff? You just know it's about us."

"Of course it is," he said, his voice revealing his smirk. "We're their favourite topic of conversation."

I snorted. "You wish. You're in the top ten, but you're not as interesting as coffee, chocolate, work, and football."

"Football! But you don't even watch football." Will's voice was in faux-wounded territory.

"I know. Now do you see?" I snorted. He slid his hands from my waist and started tickling me. I jerked around, trying to escape and push his hands off, but he was too strong. "All right. All right! I surrender. All we do is talk about you and Beren. All day." I was heavy breathing as if I'd just sprinted a mile. He relented and dropped his hands. Thank God.

"Right answer."

I rolled my eyes, since he was behind me and couldn't see. Beren and Liv both laughed. Will's phone rang. Damn. I wouldn't say I was psychic, but a bad feeling washed over me. Well, it was rarely a good thing when his phone rang because it was more often than not work related. I would bet Angelica was on the other end of the line. Will covered his other ear and spoke loudly. "Hello, yes. Hang on." Will left our group and wandered into the room we'd first entered, no doubt so he could hear what was being said.

Liv and I shared a worried look, but then I shrugged. "Come on, drink up, and then we'll dance. It's not every day your parents throw you an awesome party."

Will returned, a look I knew all too well on his face. "I'm sorry, Liv, but Angelica needs me at work. She's called me in rather than Beren so you two can enjoy tonight." He wrapped me in a hug. "Sorry, Lil. I've gotta go, but I should be home around two."

"Is that a.m. or p.m.?"

He chuckled. "A.m., I hope. Who knows, you might still be here partying."

I laughed. "You never know. A few more cocktails could lead to anything."

He gave me a quick kiss on the mouth. "Happy birthday again, Liv. Oh, and bring me home a piece of cake."

She smiled. "Will do, and stay safe. Thanks for coming." She gave him a quick hug, and he left.

Even as Liv, Beren, and I took to the dance floor, stupid Kate shooting her dagger gaze at us from the sidelines, a bucket of dread splashed over me. I shook it off because I was probably being silly, and I was determined to help Liv celebrate her birthday, but something bad was coming.

I just knew it.

CHAPTER 4

I yawned and took another sip of coffee. After what turned out to be a late night for Liv's birthday, I finally crawled out of bed at eleven thirty. Liv was already in the kitchen when I went down, and Will had gone back to work. The PIB was swamped again, and, as usual, it had come out of the blue.

Liv and I sat next to each other at the kitchen table. I gave her a sober look because this was serious. "So, tell me what Owen said last night. And don't leave anything out."

She smiled, happiness radiating too brightly for the morning after, or should that be lunchtime? "Well, he said Beren and I would have a hurdle to navigate, but once that's done, we'll be good. He also said I have scars from my past, but that I would achieve what I wanted and have closure."

"Ah, that's kind of generic information. Did he give any specifics?"

Her smile fell. "He knew I'd had a hard time at school. He brought it up. He said he could see I'd struggled at school with bullying, and that I carried that baggage, but he said not to worry, that I'd soon put it behind me."

I raised my brows. She must have been thinking about that last night because of stupid Kate. "Why did your mother ask Kate anyway? Doesn't she know you hate her?"

She shook her head. "I didn't want to burden Mum with that. She went out of her way to make it nice, and I never told her about the bullying at school. I mentioned something once, and she and Dad said not to worry, all kids go through it, that it's worse to make a big deal out of it. I figured there was no point telling them anything after that."

I frowned as sadness trickled through me. "That's terrible. I'm sorry. If I'd gone to your school, I would've definitely been your friend because you're awesome." I smiled. "You know it says more about them than you, right? And I think we've had this conversation." I chuckled. "In any case, you have me, Beren, Will, and Imani now, and we all adore you."

She smiled. "Thanks, Lily. I know, but it's hard to move on altogether. I'm okay most of the time, but every now and then something will remind me, and it's like I'm back to being fifteen again where everyone is saying cruel things, and I'm at home hating how fat I am but unable to stop eating. I worked so hard to shift that weight, and then seeing Kate again...." She sighed. "And I never really got to my goal. I'd like to lose another stone."

I sat up straight. "Don't be ridiculous! You're gorgeous

just the way you are. If you lost a stone, you'd lose your boobs, and I'm not sure that's a healthy weight. You look slim but muscular, and you have a tiny waist. I don't want you disappearing on me."

She quirked one side of her mouth up and shrugged. "Well, I was good last night. I only had one piece of cake, but all those cocktails weren't good. I'm going to hit the gym later."

"That's fine, but just don't worry about your weight. You're on the slim side already. I think you're wasting valuable brain space on stressing about it. There are better things to think about, like chocolate and Beren." I grinned.

Her smile returned, for which I was grateful. "I suppose you're right. So, what are you doing tonight? Beren has to work. I was thinking maybe you, Imani, and I can catch a movie."

"Sounds good to me. Will's working today, so who knows what time he'll be finished, and then he'll be tired."

"Great. I mean, not that Will's working, but that we can catch up." She drank the last bit of her tea and stood. "I'm going to get ready and head out. I'll text you the movie and time. Any preferences?"

"Why don't you surprise me?"

Her mouth dropped open. "But you hate surprises."

"Yeah, I know, but I'm too tired to think right now."

"Fine, but don't complain if you don't like what we see."

"Promise. Besides, I'll have Maltesers and popcorn to keep me quiet." I grinned.

She laughed. "Fine. I'll text you later. Bye." We each

waved, and she left to get changed. But she was right; I hated surprises, and there was a reason for that. Surprises, in the majority of cases, in my experience, ended up being yucky rather than pleasant. I crossed my fingers that the universe was in a happy mood and granted my wish. And yes, the optimist in me was strong—which was good, because sometimes she was all that kept me going.

Post junk-food regret engulfed me as I sat on the toilet in the movie theatre's bathroom. The fact that Imani was in the stall next to me didn't bode well for our food choices. The movie, a cheesy remake of a remake of a remake, had been terrible, and Imani and I had stomach aches. We'd not minded walking out early, something I'd never done before. What a waste of money. "That's the last time I let you choose the movie," I called from my stall to Liv, who was waiting in the hand-washing area, sans stomach ache. Lucky duck.

"Ha, no complaining. Remember?"

"Yeah, yeah." I finished up, and just before I flushed the toilet, a new voice, one I recognised, echoed from the main bathroom area.

"What are you doing here, fatty?" Liv didn't respond to Kate's taunt, and she continued. "Cat got your tongue? Oh, did you like my present?" Huh? I didn't know she'd given Liv a present, and, in fact, we hadn't even gotten around to discussing what gifts she'd gotten for her birthday. Did that make me a bad friend?

Liv's fake-nice voice was in place. "It's great, thanks. That diet and exercise journal will definitely come in handy." What the hell? Why wasn't she telling her to sod off? I wanted to flush the toilet and go and rescue her, but I was worried I'd miss hearing something.

"That's good, because you need it, fatty. Look at those rolls." A light, uncomfortable touch of magic, like the scratch of cockroach claws, touched my scalp, which was weird, considering Kate wasn't a witch, and neither was Liv. Had I imagined it, or was it some strange premonition thing? I stood and pulled my jeans up, just in case I Liv needed rescuing.

"Hey, don't touch me! Get off." And that was Liv's distressed voice.

Ah, stuff it—I flushed and yanked my door. I hurried out of the stall and into the hand-washing area just as Imani did the same. As I got there, Liv shoved Kate, who flew back, tripped, and fell. Her head made a thudding crack as she hit the tiles.

Crap.

Liv's eyes were wide. She stood deathly still, staring at the horrible woman unconscious on the floor. Imani knelt next to Kate and gently lay her hands on either side of her forehead as crimson flowed across the white tiles from under her head. My scalp vibrated with warmth.

"Can you fix it, Imani?" I asked, hoping she had some healing skills.

She shook her head. "I can only do basic stuff, like sending a bruise away or maybe a small cut. This is much worse. Not only is her skull cracked, but she has bleeding on the brain. She's still breathing, though." She withdrew her hands. I snatched my phone from my bag and rang the emergency services. I explained the situation, and they promised to have an ambulance to us ASAP. I hung up.

"Can… can you call B?" Liv's voice shook. She hadn't moved, and her dark skin had turned ashen.

"I can't." Imani stood and gave her a hug. "We can't interfere with a crime scene. If he heals her, and there's been a crime committed, he's destroying evidence."

My brow tightened. "But what if it's the only thing that saves her life? Surely, he can do something, even if it's small… just enough to help her have a good outcome? And what crime? Liv was just protecting herself." Then I had an idea. I brought up the camera app on my phone and pointed it at Kate. My breath hitched at the truth—she was see-through. I swallowed. "If we don't do something, she's dead." Imani and Liv stared at me. "My camera doesn't lie. Can you really let it go knowing this?"

Imani nodded at the security camera in the corner, mumbled something, then pulled out her phone. She dialled. "Beren, yep, it's me. We have a situation." She gave him the details, and within seconds, he was exiting from the out-of-order stall at the far end of the toilets.

"Over here," Imani called.

"Kate? Kate, where are you?" I looked at Imani. She blinked. Crap. Kate's friend from last night walked in. She took us in, then noticed who was lying on the floor. Her mouth dropped open. "Oh my God! What have you done?"

Beren ran to us at the same time Kate's friend knelt next to Kate. "Kate. Kate, can you hear me?" She tapped Kate's cheek, then screamed. "She's bleeding. You killed her! You killed her!

Beren glanced at me, alarm on his face. Before he could even check Kate out, the main door to the bathroom flung open, and two paramedics rushed in. Damn. We were too late. And it had all been captured on security camera. Beren moved out of the way so the paramedics could do their thing. Then he went to Liv and enveloped her in a hug.

Kate's friend stood, blood staining the knees of her denim jeans. She glared at Olivia and me. "You better get a good solicitor, murderers." What the hell? And why was she looking at me? Not that I wanted Olivia to take the blame either, but this idiot had no idea.

"I didn't do anything, and neither did Liv. If Kate hadn't been attacking her—"

The bathroom door opened again, and two police officers, a man and a woman, walked in. I clutched my stomach as it dove to the floor. This didn't look good at all.

The taller officer, a twenty-something-year-old with kind brown eyes stopped when he saw Liv. "Olivia?" She nodded, and I was pretty sure his question was really, "Don't tell me you're in trouble?" They likely had worked together. He frowned, his expression sad as she shrugged.

She held her hands in front of her, and the policeman

shook his head. "Just questions at this stage. So, what happened?"

"Oh, I can tell you what happened." Kate's friend stood between the police officer and Olivia.

I jumped in, wanting to defend her. "You weren't even in here, whatever your name is. Kate"—I gave a nod to the body on the floor—"was harassing Olivia. Liv was just defending herself. She pushed her away, and she fell. It was an accident."

Beren shook his head at me and pursed his lips. He must've wanted me to be quiet, but how could I not defend Liv? The second officer, youngish but female, gave me a condescending stare. "We weren't asking you." Oops, *sorry*. My face heated. I guess making them angry wasn't going to do Liv any favours, but they had to see she hadn't done anything wrong. And why pick on me? The stupid witch who hadn't even been in the room when it happened was trying to tell them what was going on.

Beren whispered something to Liv, then stood in between Liv and the police. "I've advised her not to say anything until we get a solicitor. I'm not exactly sure what happened either, but Olivia has nothing to say at this time." He fixed a serious stare onto me. "And neither does Lily."

The policewoman rolled her eyes and looked back up at the security camera. "It doesn't matter at this stage. All the information we need will be on that." She turned to us. "We'll want you at the station for questioning later." She handed me her card. "There's the address. When you come in, you can ask for me. If I'm not there, they'll assign someone else to take your witness statements. If you haven't come in by tomorrow afternoon, we'll come looking for you." She then asked for Imani and my names and contact information, which we gave her. I considered not, but that would just annoy her more and probably end up in me getting arrested or fined or something.

One of the paramedics stood and cleared his throat. The police turned and looked at him. He shook his head and looked down. I sighed, sadness and fear coalescing into a lead weight in my belly. It was true that I didn't like Kate, but I didn't want her dead, and certainly not in a circumstance that would get my best friend in trouble.

The police looked back at Olivia, and the guy said, "You'll need to come with us for questioning. I'm sorry, Olivia, but you're under arrest on suspicion of killing the deceased." He quickly looked at Kate, then back at Olivia. "You do not have to say anything, but it may harm your defence if you do not mention when questioned something which you later rely on in court. Anything you do say may be given in evidence."

She nodded, her face despondent. Shoulders sagging, she shuffled to them and let them cuff her and lead her out. I blinked back tears. This couldn't be happening. I wanted to run after them and grab my friend, steal her and travel us both somewhere far away. She didn't deserve this or the humiliation of being led through the movie theatre foyer like a common criminal for all the world to see.

Two more police officers entered the bathroom. "Time

for you all to leave. We're setting up a crime scene." The middle-aged man waved police tape in front of me.

"Why aren't you arresting her too?" Kate's friend glared at me. If she didn't shut up soon, maybe they would have to arrest me for murder. Yes, I was feeling rather aggressive, but could anyone blame me when someone was trying to have my friend and me arrested for something we didn't even do, something that was clearly an accident?

Beren looked at Imani and I as the paramedics stood to the side, allowing a forensic police officer in to take photos. At least the other police ignored Kate's friend, who put her hands on her hips and spat, "You won't get away with this. I'll make sure." She turned and stomped out.

The guy with the police tape raised a brow. "Do you think you could leave now, if it's not too much trouble?"

None of us spoke as we walked out, but our faces said it all—this was the worst night ever. Seemed the universe wasn't in a good mood, or it had something against me and my friends.

"What do we do now?" I asked, my voice almost cracking with tears.

Beren's jaw clenched, the muscles bulging. "I'm going to grab a solicitor and go to the station. Imani, if you can notify my aunt, I'd appreciate it, and Lily, just go home and wait. There's nothing you can do right now."

Well, that answer was unacceptable. "Are you sure? I mean, how the hell am I just meant to wait? My best friend's been arrested. I have to do something." Nausea bubbled up my throat. I forced it back down.

"You can come with me, love." Thank God Imani understood. I'd go mad at home by myself. "Come on then. Let's get on with it." As we made our way through the foyer, moviegoers, their hands full of popcorn, soft drink, and chocolate, stared at us, likely wondering what the hell was going on.

Well, I could tell them what was going on. A big fat nightmare none of us were going to wake up from anytime soon.

CHAPTER 5

Eight thirty the next morning, and nothing had improved. She hadn't been charged yet but was being held at the Kent police lockup until they could determine her bail conditions, which would hopefully happen on Monday. They called it pre-charge, which sounded ominous. I figured they intended to charge her, but they weren't sure what they would charge her with. Will had explained they had a choice of involuntary or voluntary manslaughter or even murder, although there was nothing premeditated about this. There was no way they could charge her with murder, could they?

"So, you didn't see what happened before she pushed her?" Ma'am leaned towards Imani and me. She and Will sat on one Chesterfield, Imani and I on the other. Beren was busy getting Liv's solicitor up to speed before they went to see her at the station.

"No," we answered in unison.

"But before I ran out, she told Kate to get off her. She was obviously just defending herself." I folded my arms. I would defend my friend to the death, or at least shout out her innocence until I'd run out of people to shout to.

Ma'am pursed her lips. "I also understand she and Kate didn't get along, that there have been a couple of incidents lately where Kate's antagonised her?"

Everyone looked at me. Of course they did. Now I had to practically dob my friend in. "Yes, but Liv took it well. I mean, I was the one telling Kate off. Liv was just upset, as in sad. She never said anything threatening, not even in private to me later."

"And you didn't know Kate was going to be at the movies?"

I shook my head. "No. Liv suggested we go, and I left it up to her to choose the movie and time."

Ma'am nodded slowly, her tone just on the wrong side of judgemental. "I see...."

My eyes widened. I'd inadvertently dropped her in hot water. Crap. But there was no way she would have known Kate would be there at that time. "Look, we didn't even see Kate when we got to the movies, and it was only that the movie was so bad that we left early. We'd travelled there, so we were having a quick toilet stop on the way out. All that soft drink, popcorn, and Maltesers will have that effect."

Will scrunched his face up. "TMI, Lily. TMI."

Okay, so I was the queen of too much information, at

times. "I'm nervous, okay? I don't want to say anything that gets Liv in trouble. She's innocent."

"So it's possible she could have known Kate was going to be there?" Ma'am pinned me with her stern gaze. I was an easy target, especially compared to veteran-agent Imani. She knew when to shut up. My brain went into blabbermouth mode at the slightest provocation.

I wiped sweaty palms on my jeans, then shrugged. Maybe I should invoke the right to remain silent, lest I incriminate Liv.

"There was something unusual." I swivelled my head around to shoot daggers at Imani. She wasn't going to put Liv further in it, was she? I couldn't believe she would. We were all friends. I liked Imani, and she was sworn to protect me. She was a good egg. She raised a brow at me. "Oh, for goodness' sake. I'm not about to say anything that would get Olivia into trouble. You know me better than that."

I sighed. "I'm sorry. I know I do. It's just…." I slouched. "This all looks so bad."

"I know, love, but Liv is the sweetest person I've ever met. There's no way she meant to hurt Kate. Anyway"—she turned back to Ma'am—"as I was saying, there was something not quite right. It's nothing I can prove, but I felt a sensation, magic maybe. It was so subtle and gone so quickly that I can't be sure. I scanned for a magic signature before we left, and there were six different ones. I can't be sure if any of them were related to what I felt. Come to think of it, it was similar to what happened at the dance recital. Also, Kate's friend came in looking for her, and she's a witch."

I sat up straighter. "I felt it too… at the movies. It was familiar, but I wasn't sure because it didn't last long at all. It could definitely have been magic. Do you think it was Kate's friend?"

Imani shrugged. "Anything's possible. But why would she want her friend to get hurt?" If Kate treated her friends like she did her enemies, I could think of plenty of reasons.

"Right. We'll leave that friend angle alone for the moment—we can always follow it up later. I want you to get back to the cinema now. Use the cubicle and no-notice spell. Record whatever's there. We'll try and match the signatures against what we found at the community centre the day of the dance." Ma'am stood. "I have to get back to headquarters, but I'll check in with you all this afternoon." She built her doorway and stepped through, disappearing.

Imani stood. "I'm off. Catch you all later."

After she left through her doorway, Will and I remained, looking at each other across the low coffee table. "Now what?" Something was niggling deep in my subconscious, but I couldn't figure it out. It was likely super important. In the meantime, maybe Will had something to offer. He stood, came around to my couch, and sat next to me.

He put his arm around me, and I snuggled into his side. "Lily?"

"Yes?"

"The night we went to see the Christmas trees at the church. You remember that?"

I half laughed. "Of course I remember; it was a week ago. I know my memory sucks, but I'm not a goldfish."

"You know fish can probably remember things for months, right?"

"Actually I didn't. Interesting. Maybe I am a goldfish, then. What about squirrels?"

"They have good memories. They can remember things for years. You'd starve if you were a squirrel. You'd forget where you left your nuts." He chuckled.

"I'm not going there. Nope." I grinned. "Anyway, what about the night we saw the trees?"

"You and Imani mentioned a weird and very quick sensation that might have been magic. I felt something like that in the church, just before that tree fell on the old lady. I didn't think anything of it at the time, but now…."

So, that was a good thing, and a bad thing. Maybe something else was at work here. But what? And how would we find out exactly, since my talent was useless—proven at the community hall. If it was magic related, the spell was an unusual one, where the caster wasn't present. We also had the problem of the magic being so faint that there was virtually nothing left to find. "I suppose it would be useless to go back to the church and look around now."

"Definitely. Any trace would be long gone. I'd be surprised if Imani finds anything at the movies."

I stopped leaning against him, pushing away quickly to sit up straight. "You don't think the snake group has anything to do with this, do you?" Just what we needed— more Dana Piranha drama. I snorted. Funny how Dana rhymed with drama, even funnier that I hadn't realised until now. Sometimes I was slow on the uptake.

"I have no idea. And what's so funny?"

"Nothing. Just my brain being stupid."

"How unusual." He shook his head.

"I couldn't pick up anything with my camera at the community hall, but maybe I should try at the church. Just in case."

"I suppose it can't hurt, and, to be honest, other than interviewing a lot of people, we have no other direction to take."

"Who would you interview, other than Kate's friend?" I wouldn't dismiss her part in this until I knew for sure. She was just as horrible as Kate, and there was no honour among thieves, as they say.

"The two men in the altercation at the church. The old lady's family. The families of the kids who were hurt at the dance recital. There might be a common thread, but at this point, I'm not sure where to start, other than with the 'do you know if anyone is out to get you' question, and my gut tells me this isn't quite like that."

The familiar niggle I'd felt in the movie toilets was back. "I feel like I'm missing something too." *Come on, subconscious. Do your thing, figure it out, and get back to me.* My stomach grumbled. I rolled my eyes. "Don't go getting jealous on me. Or are you just hungry?"

Will's brow wrinkled. "What?"

"Oh, sorry. I wasn't talking to you."

"Who the hell were you talk— Ah, your stomach?"

I grinned. It was scary how well he knew me. "Bingo!"

He laughed. "It's never boring with you; that's for sure.

So, let's go visit the church." He stood, dragging me up with him.

I magicked my camera into my hand, then set it on the floor and did the same to get my boots and jacket on. Will magicked his coat on, and we were ready. It was freezing and overcast but not raining. We strolled, holding hands. It was quite pleasant— well, except for the fact my best friend was locked up. I hoped the Kent police had less stinky cells than the PIB. The smell was almost as traumatising as being confined. "If… if they don't let her out, can we go visit Liv later?"

He squeezed my hand reassuringly. "Of course. But if it happened as you described, chances are, it will be an involuntary manslaughter charge, and she should get out on bail."

"How did we even end up in this situation? I mean, one minute you're minding your own business, and the next, someone accosts you, you react, and you're in jail?" Not to mention how Liv would feel. As much as Kate tormented her, Liv would be sick to her stomach, as I was when I killed those guys who tried to kidnap me, and Jeremy's mother. It didn't matter if the person was evil—it stayed with you.

"Wrong place, wrong time. Don't worry. Beren's grabbed the best solicitor he can, and with the video evidence, it should be cut and dried."

I wanted to believe him, but there was the matter of whether she knew Kate was going to be at the movies or not. "Just say she was found guilty of the unintentional manslaughter one. Would she go to jail?"

"Possibly, but as this is her first offence, maybe not. She might get a suspended sentence, which means she won't go to jail."

"And, not that I believe this is the case, but what if she's charged with intentional?" My stomach tensed in anticipation. Will looked down at me, his gaze assessing. "Just give it to me straight. I can handle it." I actually didn't know if I could, but nothing had been decided yet, so I just had to have faith that it would all work out.

"Somewhere between two to ten years."

The frigid air scoured my throat as I sucked in a shocked breath. This couldn't be happening. This would ruin her life. Beren would move on without her, she wouldn't be able to keep her job, and the chances of her getting another one when she got out were slim to none, not to mention the experience of being incarcerated with tough-nut criminals. That wasn't her. She wasn't a killer. As long as I'd known her, I'd never witnessed her get angry about anything, except when she was poisoned by that spelled tea. My eyes widened. Could that be it? Could someone have put a spell on her to make her more aggressive? Not that she'd been super aggressive—she'd only defended herself. But who, and why? Dana maybe? "We need to talk to Liv. I know a lot about her, but I didn't know about the teasing when she was in high school. Maybe there's someone else who's out to get her? Maybe magic caused her to push Kate harder than she'd meant to, or made Kate trip? It's not like Liv pushed her that hard." If it was caused by magic, the PIB could take over, and it would be likely the charges would be dropped since it wasn't her fault.

"Maybe. We'll have a chat with her later, okay? Until then, try not to think of all the what ifs. I know it's not easy."

"The last few months have been anything but easy. I've had plenty of practice at waiting. I'm not saying I'm any better at it than I was before, but at least I know that I can handle the excruciation of it. Not knowing what was happening with you was horrible." I looked into his battleship-grey eyes so he could see the suffering. Um, not because I wanted him to feel bad, but I wanted him to know how much I cared.

He stopped walking and pulled me in for a big hug. "Knowing you were waiting for me kept me going. You were the one light I had to hold onto." He nuzzled his cheek against mine, his stubble scratchy, but his skin and nearness warmed me both inside and out. I thanked the universe for returning him to me alive and well.

"I'm just glad you're here." I smiled up at him. "I guess we should get this over and done with." We kept walking. Soon, we'd turned a couple of corners, and there was St Mary's Church with its pretty stone walls and iconic-style arched windows. Inside was cold. Bereft of Christmas trees —the event had finished—it seemed very empty. Even though the muted winter light still illuminated the stained glass, causing a stunning, colourful glow at every window, there was nothing soft about the church. Hard floors, hard walls, no people. Well, there were two people chatting in the aisle—the priest and maybe a parishioner.

The priest looked over his companion's shoulder at us. "Can I help you?"

I smiled and jumped in. I was sure my storyline would be more plausible with my Aussie accent. "Hi. I hope you don't mind, but I'd love to take some photos and have a look around. I love old churches, especially the windows. We were here about a week ago, for the tree festival, but it was rather crowded, so I couldn't get a sense of the architecture."

He smiled. "Certainly. Have a wander around. Take your time."

"Thank you."

Will leaned down, putting his mouth near my ear to whisper. "Nice work. I should let you tag along more often." He straightened and smirked.

I rolled my eyes. "Yeah, yeah. Who's tagging along with who, Agent Crankypants?" I smiled and took the lens cap off the camera. I went back and stood near the entry. Facing the interior, I said, "Show me who used magic to hurt the old lady the other night." I pictured the incident, just to make sure my magic showed me that event, and not some random thing. Hopefully no other old ladies had been hurt here lately, but you never knew.

Nothing. Hmm. Maybe I needed to go back to basics to find some direction. I'd take anything I could get. "Show me someone casting a spell here in the last month." Whoa! That was new. Two overlapping images. I snapped two shots, then walked forward slowly, taking pictures as I went. I ended up at the pulpit end of the church, taking photos back the way I'd come. I seemed to have every angle worked out, but it would take an effort to decipher the mess. One of the pictures had Christmas trees, the other didn't, from what I could see. The jumbled images were confusing.

I had one more thing to try. "Show me someone casting a spell in the last month to hurt someone else." I couldn't say I was disappointed when nothing showed up. What a relief. I took a few photos of the stained-glass windows—just so the priest thought I was a legit sightseer. After a few more minutes of admiring the architecture—I even took a shot of the vaulted timber-lined ceiling because it was interesting, and I was only human—I gave Will the nod to leave. I called out a thank you to the priest as we left.

Once we were outside, Will asked, "Did you get anything?"

"I'm not sure. I don't think so. Wanna grab a coffee from Costa and talk about it?"

He grinned. "You left out 'and a double-chocolate muffin.'"

"Ha! That goes without saying, surely." Just the mention of my favourite junk food had me almost smelling its smooth, rich fragrance. My mouth watered.

Costa was warm and busy. We got our food and ended up at a table in the centre of the room because it was so busy. No window tables for us. "Here." I handed Will my camera so he could flick through the pictures. While he did that, I sipped my coffee and let melancholy seep over me.

This was where I'd met Liv, that day many months ago, when that stupid witch with the clawed talons was being cruel. It turned out she was actually dating Liv's fiancé, and they were both swindling money out of retirees. I sighed. We'd both had a rough year. Hadn't she been through enough already?

Will gave me my camera. "I see what you mean. That jumbled mess is almost impossible to decipher, but the point is, no one had tried to hurt anyone, so we have nothing." He sipped his coffee and stared at the table, thinking. His gaze wandered back to my face. "I think we're going to have to interview the two men from the Christmas tree event, and the family of the old lady. We have to start somewhere."

"But how could they possibly be related to what Liv is going through?"

"I don't know. Just a hunch. Besides, we've got nothing to lose. I'll have to okay it with Ma'am first. I'll drag James along too. His lie-detecting skills are second to none." I didn't know if he had the power to summon Ma'am, but his phone rang, and I'd just bet it was her. "Hello, Ma'am. Yes?" *Ha, I knew it!* His brows drew down as he listened to her. His mouth dropped open, then he contorted his face into the look you make when someone's just vomited in front of you. "Right. I'll see you there. I'll be about fifteen minutes. I'm just at Costa with Lily, and I can't go straight from here. Okay. Bye."

I grabbed my half-eaten muffin and wrapped it in a napkin before picking up my coffee, which I'd ordered in a takeaway cup. Standing, I said, "Come on. You can tell me about it on the way home."

Outside, the glacial air struck my face. If it was this cold, why couldn't it just snow? I mean, what was the fun of freezing weather otherwise? Chilly temperatures without the fluffy white stuff was like ice without the cream—bland, cold, and unsatisfying. "Spill."

"Two men in their twenties were at a local, private big-cat park. You can arrange to get up close and personal to lions, tigers, that kind of thing. One of the tigers went berserk and killed one of the men. He was a non-witch, but his boyfriend was a witch, said he felt a brief moment of magic just before the attack happened. While the big-cat place called the regular police, the witch called us."

"Have they ever had any other accidents at the park?"

"I have no idea. I'll find out soon."

"Will you let me know everything, you know, just in case any of it is similar to Liv's case?" I grabbed his arm, hugged it, and looked up at him with the best pleading gaze I could muster.

"I'll clear it with Ma'am first, but I'm sure it will be fine. Maybe we should call a meeting for this afternoon. Which reminds me, we're due to have one about the you-know-what soon." He meant the snake group, but since he was too lazy to put up a bubble of silence, he spoke in code. I imagined if they weren't listening in all the time, they might have a trigger-word alert set up, like big corporations and governments did while they spied on us from our electronic devices. And I wasn't paranoid. I'd just had too many face-to-face conversations about obscure things, like twenty-year-old books and squirrel Christmas tree ornaments to then see them advertised when I logged into social media.

I sighed loudly. "Do you ever think life will get easier? I could do with a holiday in France, or maybe Austria. I just wish everything was happy for a change. Is that too much to ask?"

Will gave me a sympathetic look and shrugged. "Well, if it never happens, it won't be for lack of trying. But first things first. Let's figure out how to clear Liv's name."

"Sounds good to me." Well, we had to start somewhere, and freeing my best friend was the best idea ever. The only problem: we had no clues. We were definitely floundering.

By the time we reached home, I realised how helpless we were and how much we were relying on Luck, and if she was as moody as the universe, things were going to get messy.

CHAPTER 6

We sat around a PIB boardroom table in our usual meeting room. Beren, who sat opposite me and next to my brother, was in the middle of explaining why we couldn't go and see Liv. "She's asked for no visitors, except for me and the solicitor. I'm sorry."

"That's ridiculous." I tried to keep the irritation out of my voice, but Beren raised a brow, indicating I probably hadn't succeeded. "She needs us, and I need to see her, make sure she's okay."

"I know, Lily, but that was her request. I think she's still trying to process all this, and to be honest, she's in self-hate mode right now. She blames herself and thinks she deserves to be in jail." Beren ran a hand through his blond hair, mussing it. "She's lost her appetite and just lies in her bed. The only times she gets up is when I visit, which has only been twice. The Kent police are being as nice as they can, but unless I have the solicitor with me, they're not going to let me in five times a day. Anyway, they're holding her for an extra twenty-four hours while they gather more evidence."

"What, they're still not sure what to charge her with?" I looked at Beren, my face showing every bit of incredulity vibrating in my body. "She clearly didn't intend to hurt Kate. I mean, if I pushed someone away, I would never do so thinking they were going to fall and smash their head. If I wanted to do some damage, I'd at least punch them first."

James fixed a worried gaze on me. "Since when did you get so violent?"

I waved one hand. "I'm not. I just mean, who ever thinks pushing someone is going to kill them, unless they're standing next to a cliff, of course? This whole thing is ludicrous." I folded my arms with angry enthusiasm. My frustration was rising. While we sat there discussing things, Liv was in a tsunami of self-hate and despondency. Did she believe she was going to go to jail for ten years? I wished I could say I didn't know how horrific that felt. Maybe knowing made it worse.

"Yes, it is ludicrous, dear, but it's the situation we have. Rather than ranting about it, maybe we should better use our time to brainstorm how to fix it?" Ma'am had her teacher voice activated—mildly scathing yet calm.

Instead of answering, I pushed my aggravation out in a huge blast of air through my nose. It was times like this I wished I was a dragon shifter. I knew they didn't exist, but they should. Then I could burn everything to the ground, get Liv out of there. Hmm, maybe that's why dragon shifters didn't exist—too many things would get burnt to a crisp. I could imagine driving along and you let someone cut in front of you, and they don't even wave a thank you. Instead of swearing, I could engulf their car in flames. Hmm, maybe I was getting violent. I needed to calm down before I lost the plot and ended up in jail with Liv.

Will squeezed my hand. "Just be patient. We'll get to the bottom of this." He turned to Ma'am, who was sitting on his left. "I think it's time to update everyone on this morning's case." She nodded. Will turned to address the rest of the table. "The man mauled to death this morning at the big-cat park had been living his dream. His partner told us that he'd always wanted to interact up close with big cats. He was feeding the tigers this morning with park staff present. Everything was going well, and he leaned in to pat one, which also went well—that tiger has been declawed and is tame, having been brought up from a kitten."

"Declawing is cruel." I knew I should let him talk, but I just had to get that out there.

"Yes, Lily, it is, but that's not the point." Will shook his head. "As I was saying… everything was going well, but then, after being warned not to smother the animals, the man's partner, Alfred, says he felt a hiss of magic. Then his boyfriend, after promising not to, leaned in to hug the tiger. It didn't take kindly to that and mauled him. It all happened so quickly that Alfred didn't have time to use his magic to save Irving. He was also aware that the owners of the park were non-witches, and he would have had some explaining to do, but he says he would have used his magic had he been thinking clearly. We obviously would have done damage control because saving a life is a special circumstance." It was nice to know the PIB weren't absolutely cruel when it came to enforcing the no-magic-in-front-of-non-witches law. "We couldn't find a magic signature, but Alfred assures us there was a faint golden aura around Irving just before he died. It wasn't there by the time we arrived."

I scratched my head. There were definite similarities with this, the church case, the dance case, and Liv's. The brief pulse of magic was present at all of them, although I hadn't seen a golden aura around anyone at the movies. "Imani, did you notice any golden auras at the dance recital?"

She shook her head. "I wasn't looking with my other sight. Seeing auras all the time gets overwhelming, especially in a dark hall. The brightness would've been distracting."

I knew what she meant. I only checked out people with my other sight if I needed to know whether someone was a witch or not. Ma'am had finally taught me how to block it out without turning my magic off. I looked at Will. "Did Alfred tell you anything else?"

"No, but he was distraught. We're going to try and talk to him again tomorrow. We did ask if any witches had it in for either of them, but he said no. So, whilst we haven't found the source of these pulses of power, we've established a common theme in these incidents. Now it's time to dig deeper, see what else we can discover."

James jumped in. "To that end, this afternoon, Will and I will interview the two men and the old lady's family from the Christmas-tree incident. I think we can assume the source of these crimes is coming from a single person or group." He looked at me when he said "group." Regula Pythonissam had been unusually quiet the past few weeks. Maybe they were regrouping, or maybe they'd been making more mischief like this. "In the meantime, Lily, you need to go home and wait. I'm sorry, but there's nothing more you can do right now, and you never know—Liv might change her mind and decide she wants to see you this afternoon or tomorrow."

"Could I go and visit Millicent?" My sister-in-law was about five or six weeks from giving birth. The baby was due in January. Maybe she needed help with the housework. Oh, that's right, she was a witch and could just magic everything clean. Well, maybe she'd like the company. I sure as hell could use it.

"I'm sure she'd love to see you. Just text her first to make sure she's not asleep. She still hasn't been sleeping well at night. Our baby loves to kick up a storm at two in the morning." He grinned. He couldn't wait to be a dad, and he doted on Millicent when he wasn't at work. Unfortunately, he couldn't sleep for her, so she was tired most of the time.

I pulled out my phone and texted her right then and there. If she was up for visitors, I'd go straight there. Going back to an empty house, one that should have held Olivia, was just a depressing reminder. While Ma'am wrapped up the meeting, my phone vibrated with a message. I grinned.

Hey, Lily. Yes, please come over. I'm bored senseless. I've already watched two movies today and dozed for about an hour. I would LOVE some company. See you soon xx.

"And that's it for today, team. We'll reconvene tomorrow afternoon." Ma'am stood and left via the normal door.

Will and I stood. He smiled, but there was no kiss or hug, which was fine. I felt just as awkward as he did getting smoochy at work. It wasn't the place. "See you tonight. I should be home around seven. Maybe I'll bring some Indian takeaway with me."

Yum. My stomach gurgled happily. "Hear that? That's the sound of a stomach with something to look forward to. See you tonight."

Everyone left, and I set the coordinates to my brother's house on my door, then stepped through. As I arrived in their reception room, I remembered something I'd bought for Millicent. Her friend was having the baby shower in January, which was kind of late if you asked me—what if the baby came early? So I had another present for the baby, but I wanted to give her this now, so she had something to look forward to after the birth, other than the baby, of course. There was also something super special, something I was quite proud I'd thought of.

I accessed the river of magic. "A present for Millicent is sitting on my desk. Please send it to me post-haste." It kind of had some poetry about it. I giggled. If magic only worked with rhyme, I would have been in big trouble. An envelope and a rectangular, paperback-sized present wrapped in golden paper with storks flying across it popped into my hand. I grinned, my stomach aflutter. I was so excited to give this to her. I probably should've waited for James to be around, but I needed cheering up, and seeing her reaction would definitely go some way to making my day better.

I knocked on the reception-room door. Millicent answered it, a huge smile on her face. "Lily! It's so good to see you." She enveloped me in an awkward hug. I was kind of standing at her side. Baby bumps were an awesome way to reclaim personal space, but you had to sacrifice your body and harbour a parasite for the privilege—yes, it was going to be a lovable, cute parasite, but still.

"You look gorgeous. And look at how big the bump is." I grinned. "Not long now."

"It's still a few weeks away, which is too long if you ask me." She shut the door. "Come on through." She led me through the living area to the kitchen. It was a gorgeous addition they'd done soon after moving in. It had high raked ceilings with exposed timber beams.

I sat at the gold flecked, fawn-coloured breakfast bar, on a white stool that spun. I swivelled it from side to side and smiled. "These stools are fun."

She laughed. "You're not the only one who does that as soon as they sit there. You and your brother are so alike in some things, yet so different in others."

"Don't be too hard on him. It's not his fault he can't be as awesome as me." I smirked. She laughed again. "So, these are for you." I handed her the presents. "You have to open them now because I have to know if you like them… because it's all about me." She grinned at my joke, but honestly, where was the fun in giving if you couldn't see the happiness of the person receiving the present? I loved making people happy.

She opened the envelope first. "Oh my goodness. Thank you! I'm so going to enjoy this once the baby's out. My shoulders have been so tight because I've had to sleep on my side. If you sleep on your back it's dangerous when the baby gets this big, and obviously I can't sleep on my stomach—not that I get much sleep anyway. And James is useless when it comes to giving massages. He gets tired after two minutes. 'My hands are sore.'"

I chuckled. "He's just a big baby sometimes. I'd like to see him carry this bundle of *joy* around."

"Yes, *joy*. I love it when it kicks, and I talk to it all the time, but the rest of it I can do without."

"Okay, so don't keep me in suspense. Open the next one." I stopped swivelling the chair and bounced one knee up and down. I even had a little pod of anticipatory butter-flies flitting around the bottom of my stomach.

She tore the paper off—a woman after my own heart; who had time to be careful when there were goodies involved? She chucked the paper on the breakfast bar and looked at the present. She blinked, and two lines appeared at the top of the bridge of her nose. Tears glistened in her eyes, which made me well up too. After a minute, she found words. "How? This is incredible. Oh my God, you used your talent." She shook her head, incredulous. "This is the best present ever." She looked up at me, still shaking her head; then a beautiful smile broke out, and it was like the sun's rays coming through after a storm. She came around the table and gave me another hug. She placed the picture on the breakfast bar so we could both see it.

It was a picture of James on one knee, looking up at her. She had one hand over her mouth, and joy shone from her eyes as her other hand accepted a small box from him. The scene was backlit by a gorgeous sunset. Windswept long grass surrounded them with the ocean beyond. "But how did you know where?"

"James, of course. When he called to tell me you were getting married, I asked him a gazillion questions. Imani came with me, for safety reasons, and I took them. My talent has to be good for something other than crime solving. I took a couple of others, which I'll give you later, but this was the best one."

"Well, Lily, I don't think anything could top that present. Does James know?"

I grinned. "Nope."

"I can't wait to show him." She picked the picture up again and shook her head, still disbelieving. Mission accomplished. I'd even forgotten about the mess Liv was in for ten minutes. *Poor Liv.* I frowned. "What's wrong?"

"Just Liv's situation. One minute we're celebrating her birthday, the next she's in jail accused of killing someone." And my talent couldn't help. I sighed.

Millicent cast a bubble-of-silence spell. "Do you think it's Regula Pythonissam?"

"I really don't know. It could be. But wouldn't they

threaten me directly, let me know they're trying to get to me through my friend?"

"Maybe they want her in jail before that happens? If they warn you too early, we'll have a better idea of where to look for clues, and it could ruin everything for them."

"I have no idea. James and Will are interviewing some people this afternoon in relation to one of the other similar situations. Maybe they'll glean something from that?"

"What exactly is happening? Oh, and would you like a tea or coffee?"

"A cappuccino would be nice." I smiled. "There's a little pulse of power, which isn't strong enough to grab a signature from, and then something bad happens. All the victims are non-witches. Some guy got torn apart by a tiger this morning." I shuddered. "But then, some of the other crimes have been mild, like kids spraining their ankles."

Millicent magicked a coffee for me and a tea for her. They appeared on the breakfast bar. "Who benefits from the outcomes?"

I shrugged. "Well, um, I don't know if anyone benefits from the guy dying this morning. Kate not being around benefits Liv because she won't have to worry about running into her, but I imagine if she's that evil, there are probably others who could benefit, but killing someone so they don't bully you is a bit extreme, especially when Liv has had little to do with her over the last few years. I guess the kid who won the dance competition benefits from the other kids hurting themselves. And the woman dying by Christmas tree...." I made a "who knows" face.

"The old lady may have been rich. Maybe someone inherited something? It wouldn't be the first time money was a motive for murder."

I sipped my coffee. "But then, there are all these different reasons. There's no commonality. Do you think there's a witch cursing people for money?"

"That's a possibility."

Hmm, there was that nudge from my brain again. There was something there, but I was missing it.

A thunderous boom exploded. The house shook. Magical energy crackled around us and dissipated. We stared at each other. "What the hell was that?" I asked, throwing up my return-to-sender spell.

Millicent held her baby bump, and worry lines etched her forehead. "A magical attack."

Crap. I jumped up and looked out her kitchen window. There was no way I was going outside though, like those idiots in horror movies. "Do you want to travel to the PIB?"

"No. That's what they'd want us to do. We're safe in here. Whatever that was, it couldn't breach the spells protecting the house. The noise was the powers colliding, but they threw a lot at us—the louder the noise, the bigger the collision. They may have done that on purpose to scare me into travelling, but if they have a catch spell activated, they could send us wherever they want."

"What the hell? What's a catch spell? No one's told me about those."

"They're almost impossible to do. They take a lot of power, but also, you have to hold the magic in place while you wait for someone to travel, and the spell takes twenty or thirty minutes to set up, so you can't exactly do it on short notice. Because we know I'm a liability at the moment, with the baby and all, we check for that spell before we leave the house anyway. Hang on." She shut her eyes and mumbled something, then waved her hands. I felt a ping of magic. She flinched and opened her eyes. "Yep. There's a catch spell waiting. Scumbags."

"That sounds like a complicated spell. Honestly, I should know about those. I'm surprised I haven't been scooped up already." I thought of all the times the snake group tried to kidnap me, and Dana's hatred of me. They'd definitely had plenty of opportunity to grab me travelling from Angelica's.

"Don't worry. I'm sure Angelica has an alarm spell activated for that. We haven't put one on because we have too many other spells. It's taking a **PIB** team energy to keep the spells activated."

My mouth dried. And I'd thought I'd had a lot to worry about before. This was making my head spin. "Should we tell James?"

She nodded and went to the other end of the kitchen, to a small two-seater table against the wall. She grabbed her phone and called James. When she got off the call, she came back and sat at the breakfast bar. "He's sending some agents around to check the perimeter."

"Thank goodness. Can you teach me that spell, the one to check for it?"

"I'm not sure if now's the time. It's kind of like when you check someone's aura for their defences, like return to sender, only you have to push your magic outwards, past the walls and ceiling, past the house. If any spells are hovering out there, you'll bump into them. Once your magic touches them, the spell symbol will appear in your mind. You have to be able to decipher them, of course, and you have to be gentle in your prodding. If you hit the magic too hard, it will be like running head first into a brick wall. It hurts, and it's dangerous. That's probably why Angelica hasn't told you about all this—she knows you'd try and help, but without more experience, you might get hurt, and, well, we don't want anything happening to you." Her caring smile did nothing to soften the blow from the hammer of guilt for being a burden, or the knife of inadequacy that sliced across my ego. That was one more thing I was determined to learn, but now wasn't the time—if anything happened to me, it would endanger Millicent even more. We'd just have to ride this out, and I'd get Angelica to teach me later.

Banging sounded from the living area. "That must be them." Millicent slid awkwardly off the stool and went to answer the reception-room door. The cavalry had arrived. Thank God.

After a few minutes, Millicent returned, a uniform-clad Imani in tow. "Hey, love." She gave me a brief hug. "Just checking things out." She did a lap of the room, then pulled her gun out, opened the laundry door, and went through. Crap, that made it look way more serious. Normal British police didn't carry guns, but the PIB were a unit unto themselves. She called out, "I'm just checking out the back garden. Be back soon."

My phone rang, and I started, my heart racing. This afternoon was going to be the death of me. So much for trying to distract myself from all the bad stuff. I pulled the phone out of my bag. The name on the screen made my heart gallop out of control. "Hey, B. Have you got news?" I tensed my stomach. *Please be good news. Please be good news.*

"Sorry, but it's not good news." *Damn.* He paused, and I swallowed and shut my eyes. "They've charged her with intentional manslaughter." My eyes shot open. "Bail is set at two hundred thousand pounds. Because her parents are rich, they consider her a flight risk."

"What the hell? Don't they know you're a witch, and you could take her anywhere for free, for goodness' sake. And *intentional!* There's no way she meant to hurt her, let alone kill her. What are we going to do? Are her parents posting bail? Can she come home? I have some money saved up, if her parents don't have it. I mean, it's not that much, but maybe we could pool our money or something. Please tell me she won't be spending any more time in jail while she's waiting to go to trial. Crap."

"I know this is hard, Lily. But we'll figure this out. Her parents are going to put the money up, and she's being released into their custody. Part of the bail conditions are that she moves back in with them. She has to surrender her passport, and she can't leave the country, of course. She has to check in with the parole officers twice a week as well. If she misses an appointment, they'll issue a warrant for her arrest, and they lose their bail money."

My returning breakfast burnt my throat, and tears

scalded my eyes. I didn't trust myself to speak without crying.

"Lily, are you still there?"

"Mm-hmm." I sniffed. My voice came out in a whisper. "Tell her I'll come by tonight, whether she wants me to or not."

"Okay. I'll stay with her until then, see if we can figure out how this happened, and get the charges dropped or moved to the PIB. I'll see you at her parents' tonight."

"Okay. Bye." I put my phone on the breakfast bar and bit a nail. This was turning into a nightmare.

Millicent placed her hand on my shoulder. "Did she get charged with intentional manslaughter?"

I nodded, unable to speak. I hated crying in front of people, and I was sure I'd burst into tears if I opened my mouth for any reason.

"Well, that's just wrong. But we all know Liv's a kind soul. We just have to cross our fingers that the team can find some connection to those magical pulses. And, yes, James told me all about it." She rubbed my back as Imani came in.

Imani hurried over. "Are you all right, Lily? Don't worry. There's no one outside."

Millicent shook her head. "I'm afraid that's not why she's upset." As Millicent told Imani what had happened, I listened, still disbelieving. It was like being in the twilight zone. And for once, I had no idea how to fix it. My talent was no help for the first time ever.

Now what?

CHAPTER 7

After spending the afternoon at Millicent's, making sure she was okay, and, if I was honest, making sure I was okay, Imani came with me to grab some flowers. She was joining me to see Olivia. We figured that together, we might be able to make some headway. Liv might give us a clue without even realising, as in, something she thought was insignificant might prove valuable. After ensuring the catch spell was gone, we travelled to Imani's flat and got in her car. We couldn't travel to Liv's parents, as they had no idea witches existed, plus we needed to stop off at the shops.

Inside Parker's Blooms, enveloped in the heady fragrance of lilies and roses, we picked a gorgeous, colourful arrangement that was sure to cheer Liv up, at least a little bit. The middle-aged woman at the counter was giggling at her dark-haired male customer, who had his back to us.

"Oh, my. Thank you. I don't normally like to bother celebrities, but I just had to get your autograph. My brother had a reading at one of your shows about six weeks ago, and everything you said came true!"

The voice was familiar, and dare I say it, more arrogant than self-assured. "But of course, Miss Parker." Owen the Oracle.

Her hand fluttered at her chest. "Oh, you can call me Rosie." Ha! Rosie owned a flower shop. Who woulda thunk it?

"Well, it was lovely to meet you, Rosie, but alas, I must depart. I have a hot date." He turned, and our gazes met. The ever so slight widening of his eyes indicated he recognised me, but he was pretending he didn't.

As he walked past, I said, "Do you ever warn people? You predicted my friend's future, and you failed to mention she'd be arrested for manslaughter." My mouth dropped open. I had not expected to say that—think it, yes. But that was me, unpredictable even to myself. These scammers who told people's fortunes needed to be brought down a peg. Scammer, charging thousands of dollars for an airy-fairy service. Yes, people didn't have to buy into it—literally—but they preyed on people's vulnerabilities. Who didn't want to hear life was going to be awesome? Shame he couldn't have told her to be careful because someone was out to get her.

He stopped and slowly turned to face me. "I'm sorry. Do I know you?"

You got to be kidding me. "Not well, but you *predicted*"—

I used finger air quotes—"fortunes at my friend's birthday a couple of nights ago. And you did a dismal job."

The woman behind the counter was blinking rapidly, her face slack as hamster wheels spun in her head. She probably didn't want a smackdown between her customers, but she had no idea how to deal with the confrontation. Imani tugged my sleeve. "Lily, I think we should just buy those flowers and go." My cheeks had heated with anger, and Owen's dark eyes had darkened further—a warning for me to leave it alone?

"I can assure you, miss, that what I do is accurate and amazing. There's a reason I'm a celebrity in the field, and I can charge a premium. I tell people what they want to hear, and that's it. No one wants to know the bad things. I spread joy. People love me and will continue to do so. I've worked hard to get where I am, and no nonsensical young woman is going to change that. Good day." He swooshed around dramatically, head held high, and strode out the door.

Imani grabbed the boxed arrangement off me and set it on the counter while I stared after him. What an ass—and I meant it in the donkey form of the word. Imani's voice drifted to me. "You'll have to excuse my friend. She's going through a very stressful time. I'm sorry about that."

"Oh, yes… of course. It could happen to anyone." Her tone suggested she didn't believe a word she'd just said. "That'll be forty-two pounds."

I turned, hand in my bag to pull out the money, but Imani had already passed over her credit card. "Hey, wait. Here's some money."

"Don't be silly, love. I've got this." She waved me away. While she finished paying, I grabbed twenty-one pounds out of my wallet. I knew she wouldn't accept it now, but I'd sneak it into her pocket or car when she wasn't looking. I hated not paying my share.

Imani grabbed the flowers, and we headed out to the car. Once we'd gotten in, she turned to me, raising the pretty arrangement slightly. "Can I trust you with these?"

"Huh? What do you mean?"

"Just making sure you're not still angry. Wouldn't want you accidentally crushing them." She smirked.

I rolled my eyes, and she laughed. I shrugged and held out my hands. She raised a brow. Who knew you could have a long conversation without speaking? I held in my laugh and nodded. She gave me the flowers, and I placed them gently on my lap. But I had to speak, because, well, my mouth didn't like to be left out. "Don't worry. I'll be careful."

She started the car, checked the road, and pulled out. "So, what happened in there?"

"If he's such a genius fortune teller, how could he not warn Liv? Maybe tell her not to go to the movies in the near future. Honestly, he took thousands of dollars from her parents, and he gave her dud information."

"Maybe he wasn't looking for it, so he didn't see it. He did ask me to name a specific thing I wanted to know about. I mean, if he laid out your whole future, it would have to take hours, if not days. He wouldn't have time."

"Did he tell you anything negative?" My tone came out

accusatory. I still didn't like him.

"Well... no."

"Right. He only told me positive stuff too. And honestly, if he'd have warned me about the movies, maybe I would've listened."

"Ah, but see. Maybe you wouldn't have believed him."

"Even so, at least it would be balanced information. I think he's full of crap. Not to mention, I felt some magic. I don't know what he was doing with it, but I don't like him."

"I felt it too. It's probably just to make the experience seem more real. Or maybe he's like my mum, and it's his talent?"

"Well, he should be more careful with the information he gives. He could be helping people if he wanted. He said people only want to hear good things, so he's just doing it to be popular and have that positive association in people's minds." I stared out the window, into the late-afternoon gloom, scowling. We'd stopped at traffic lights, and a woman walking a dog thought I was glaring at her. She stuck her finger up at me. Oh my God! I started laughing.

"What's so funny?"

I told Imani, and she laughed too. If only there was going to be more laughter later, but I knew there would likely be tears.

As we drove along Liv's driveway, darkness had replaced the twilight. Gee, it got dark early here. Quarter to five in the afternoon, and I felt like it was time for dinner. As I reached for the door handle, Imani said, "Lily, go easy on the fortune-teller thing tonight. Liv's been through enough, and she doesn't need us getting overly emotional or angry, especially about something she enjoys. Okay?" She stared at me, authority in her gaze.

I pursed my lips, then huffed out of my nose. "Fine. But only because I love Liv, and I don't want to upset her any more than she already is. But I can't guarantee I won't get emotional. It's who I am."

She smiled. "I know. And that's one thing I love about you. You wear your heart on your sleeve, but remember, Liv's going to take everything we say to heart. We want to give her hope, not make her situation sound even more depressing than it already is. Right now, if we can't find what's going on, she will be going to jail. The only question is, will it be for two years, or ten."

I swallowed the nausea rising in my throat. If that happened, I didn't know what I'd do. "Right, well, we better not let it get that far." I opened the door and stepped into the frigid air. And where was the snow? It shouldn't be so cold if it wasn't going to snow. *Gah, Lily, you don't need something else to get upset about.*

Imani knocked, and Liv's dad answered. His wan smile reminded me of how I felt on a drizzling afternoon—tired and lacklustre. "I'm so glad you ladies are here. Liv needs all the support she can get." He stood aside, and in we went. His comment surprised me because the English generally weren't open with their feelings, especially when it came to people who weren't part of the family. This situation had obviously rattled everyone, which was to be expected.

We walked through to the living area at the back of the

house—the same one that'd had Owen's tent in it. The room was back to normal—no bats, no tent, and no canapes. I was going to miss those canapes.

A forlorn Liv sat on the couch, and even though it hadn't been that long since I'd seen her, she looked like she'd lost weight. Her face had thinned slightly, and her boobs were smaller—and don't get me wrong; I didn't make a habit of staring at women's boobs, but that was one of the first places people lost weight, and I just happened to notice. The stress had already taken its toll. I frowned.

Beren sat on one side of Liv and her mum, the other. Both held one of Liv's hands. She gave Imani and me a half-hearted smile. "Hey."

"Hey," we both said.

Liv's mum stood. "Thanks for coming. Would you like a cup of tea?"

"I'm fine, thanks," I said.

Imani smiled. "None for me, thanks."

"Well, I need to get started on dinner. I'll leave you lot to chat. If you want anything, just let me know." She ran a gentle hand over Olivia's head and went to the kitchen.

Imani sat in a small armchair that was near the lounge, and I took Liv's mother's place at her side. Beren looked at Imani, then me. "So, I was just explaining to Liv that we don't have any strong leads yet, but there's something we're following up."

I leaned forward. "Those interviews?"

"Yes. And Liv's lawyer, Phillip Brown, and I watched the security video from the bathroom today. It clearly shows that

Liv was taken by surprise and was acting in self-defence. The only reason they've slapped the intentional manslaughter charge is that they're saying she knew Kate was going to go, and Kate's friend reckons they agreed to meet up at the movies on the night of Liv's party."

My mouth dropped open. "But that's a lie!"

Imani looked at Liv. "It is a lie, isn't it? And before you think I'm blaming you, I'm not. I just want all the facts so I can help." Imani's voice was calm, soothing even.

Liv sniffed and nodded. "I know you're not blaming me, and of course I didn't agree to go to the movies with them. That would be my worst nightmare. But the police won't believe me. They said if I didn't like her, how come she was invited to my party." She stared at the ground. "Now Mum blames herself."

I shook my head. "It's not her fault. She was just trying to do what she thought was going to make you have the best birthday ever. The only person to blame is Kate, for bullying you, and her skanky sidekick for telling tall tales." I gritted my teeth. How I'd love to lock her in jail for a few days and see how she liked it. I shook my head. What the hell had Liv ever done to them? Why were some people lower than low? And how was it they were still alive when they didn't have a functioning heart?

"We're getting a bit off track." Imani leaned forward. "I know this is hard, Liv, but we need you to answer some questions. While the PIB are doing an official investigation into some other crimes with one similar detail, our investigation of your case is off the record since it's being handled by

Kent police. Lily and I want to follow some things up and do what we can to get this over with as quickly as possible. Are you up to answering questions tonight?"

She raised forlorn eyes. "Yes. I've spent enough time crying and feeling sick. I know I did nothing wrong, and I want to clear my name. I mean, I know I pushed her, but there's no way I wanted to hurt her, let alone kill her. It was an accident. A very unlucky accident."

My subconscious gave me a shot of déjà vu. *Unlucky.* There was something in that—I just didn't know what. Damn my subconscious brain for being so shy. Why couldn't it just come out and talk to my normal brain? Was that what the non-subconscious part was called? I had no idea. Or was it the superconscious, or the uberconscious? Oh… it was probably the conscious brain. Der. Seemed like neither part was working properly, which meant everything was normal. Right.

I gave Imani a quick glance, then turned to Olivia. "Liv, the night of your birthday, did Owen give you any indication this would happen? What did he tell you about your future?" We hadn't had an in-depth conversation about it, and when we glossed over it earlier, I knew she hadn't told me everything, probably because it was just dreamy stuff about her relationship with Beren.

"Lily," Imani warned.

"It's okay. I just need to know."

She rolled her eyes, then gave me a speedy glare as a reminder to stay cool.

Liv opened her mouth, then closed it. Beren squeezed

her hand. "It's okay, Liv. We've already been through this, and you've got nothing to be embarrassed about. They know you'd want to know about us." He smiled. "But you should've just asked me. I would've told you we're going to be together for a very long time." He brought her hand to his lips and kissed it. He was such a sweetie. I smiled. They were so cute together.

Liv took a deep breath and licked her lips. "Um, he said Beren and I would stay together, that we had a future, and that he would come to my rescue. I didn't ask anything about that because I assumed he meant just sticking up for me against Kate, or even that it was that he *saved* me after my disaster with Ernest. And I know he didn't really save me because I was fine anyway, but you know how people think, so if Owen saw I'd had a bad relationship, he may have thought of it that way."

"So he didn't warn you about anything?"

She shook her head. "Not that I can remember, and trust me, I've been over everything he said to me about one thousand times. He said I was good at my job, and that I had loyal friends. He said I was going to get a promotion at work one day. And he did see my past problems. He told me that I'd been engaged, but it didn't work out and that I'd had a great loss."

I tried so hard, but I couldn't help it; I rolled my eyes. "Could he have researched that? I mean, he knew your full name, and it did make the news at the time." Local Finance Manager Killed in Shootout with Police After Embezzling Millions from Unsuspecting Retirees was one headline.

Imani's chair must have been too far away because she looked at me, and a familiar tingle of magic shivered across my scalp, then something pinched my thigh. I jumped. "Ow!" I narrowed my eyes and scowled at her. She raised a brow as if to say, *I warned you.*

I sniffed. "When you least expect it, Imani...."

"We're not here to verify where he gets his information, Lily. We're assuming he has a talent for what he does." Imani turned to Liv. "Did you talk about anything else?"

She bit her lip. "Um, I don't think it's relevant, but I was upset, you know, after Kate brought up the past. I didn't even mention anything, but he said he sees what the cosmos shows him." Okay, so I eye-rolled again. Calling it the cosmos was so pretentious. What was wrong with the universe, or just "my crystal ball?" "He told me my weight's been an issue, and that I didn't have to worry, that because I was older, my metabolism had sped up, and I would never get fat again. And, in fact, I'd have to be careful I didn't lose too much weight."

Okay, so I'd give him that, unless he did see she was headed for hell, and she'd feel so sick about it, she couldn't eat. I eyeballed Imani, and she met my gaze, a cautioning eyebrow raised. *Hmph.* This time, I folded my arms and kept my opinion to myself.

"And that's it. We didn't talk about anything else." Liv sat back into the couch, likely relieved that question time was over.

I turned to her. "And how are you feeling? I mean, I

know you're upset, but are you holding up okay? You look like you've lost weight."

"I've hardly eaten anything since this began. My stomach's literally been in knots. Being in jail was scary and lonely and horrible, but it's not knowing what's going to happen that's the worst. Plus, as much as Kate was horrible to me, I feel bad about what happened. Her family must be devastated. If it wasn't for me pushing her, she'd still be alive." She pressed her lips together, and a tear spilled over onto one cheek.

I grabbed her other hand. "It was *not* your fault. If she hadn't touched you, intimidated you, basically assaulted you, you wouldn't have had to push her off. She brought this on herself."

"Here, here," said Imani.

Beren gave a nod. "Lily's right. And we'll prove that in court. Don't worry. There's no way I'm going to let you go to jail."

If only Beren had the power to make that happen without actually using his power. I was pretty sure he wouldn't manipulate anything in court, like the jury's decision-making process. Would he? If he did and Angelica found out, she'd put him in jail—I had no doubt. And as much as we were all desperate to see Liv exonerated, Beren wasn't dishonest. We all had to trust in the system. The thing that bothered me, though, was that the process sometimes got it wrong, and innocent people were locked up.

Liv shrugged. "I don't know, B. At this point, it's in fate's hands. I know I shouldn't think like that, but how did this even happen? Right now, I feel like the unluckiest person on the planet, well, other than Kate, of course. I suppose I should look on the positive side—I'm still here. She never gets to be anywhere again."

Now I was tearing up. "It's not your fault. You're the nicest person I know. You don't have an aggressive bone in your body. Beren's right: we'll get you out of this. We just have to make sure the jury sees all the facts."

"But they'll bring up that she teased me for years, and that I hated her, that I snapped and took my opportunity to kill her."

"Well," said Imani, "they're going to have to prove, beyond a reasonable doubt, that you meant for her to die when you pushed her, and from what Beren says, the video proves otherwise."

Beren nodded. "It sure does."

The warmth of magic cascaded over my scalp, and I jerked my head around to look at Imani. "Don't pinch me again! I didn't do anything."

She started, her hand in her handbag. "Hey, love, don't get your knickers in a twist. I was just getting this." She pulled out a framed photograph. "I forgot and left it at home." She winked and handed it to Liv. "This is for you."

The picture was from Liv's birthday. Beren stood in the middle, Liv scooped in his arms, her legs dangling over one of his arms, and her arm around his neck. I stood on one side, and Imani on the other. Our grins were huge and maybe slightly alcohol-induced, but it was clear that we were having the best time. "Whenever you feel sad, look at this and remember how much we all love you. We know you're innocent, and we won't stop till we've proven it."

Her small smile was better than nothing, but it wasn't big enough for my liking. Looked like we had our work cut out for us in the coming weeks. We'd have to be as supportive as possible, and I'd do my best to think of how we could distract her.

"Lily?"

I turned to Imani. "Yes?"

She lowered her voice. "When I started my spell, you weren't looking at me."

"No. I was looking at Beren." I scrunched my forehead. Weird question.

"Did you see my aura glow in your periphery?"

"No. I have my other sight turned off. It's too distracting seeing extra lights."

"So how did you know it was me?"

I whispered, "You mean the spell?" She nodded. "Um, I just did." Then I thought about it. It hadn't always been that way, but during the last few weeks, ever since I'd recovered from almost dying, I could tell who was using their magic from the feel of it. I hadn't even realised. "I can tell now. Everyone's feels different. Like, Angelica's has a feeling of impatience, if that makes sense. Yours is mellow and confident. Beren's is kind and strong. Hmm, sort of like your personalities." I shrugged.

Her eyebrows raised. "I told you, you were special. Honestly, you keep surprising me."

Beren leaned forward to look at me past Liv. "That's a

rare skill, Lily. Only around 10 percent of witches can feel the differences in magic."

I gasped and sat up straight. "Oh my God, that's it! The ping of magic."

"Shhhhh!" Liv's eyes were wide, and she flicked her gaze to the door from the kitchen.

I slapped my hand over my mouth, then lowered it. "Sorry. I got carried away. But remember at the church we were saying there was a ping?" Liv and Beren nodded. "The night of your party, the feel of Owen's you-know-what, and that day in the bathroom. They all felt the same." So that's what my subconscious was trying to tell me. Wow.

"Are you sure?" Beren's brow was as wrinkled as Will's usually was.

I smiled. "Yep. Positive."

Imani cocked her head to the side. "Are you sure, or is this more of your little thing against our oracle friend?"

"I swear it's not. Can you tell the difference between different people's you-know-what? Because if you can, think back to the dance competition, and then think about Liv's birthday."

She shook her head. "I can't. And how do you even prove it? We can't just assume what you're saying is right and act on it without some kind of proof."

Liv's mum came through the door. "Dinner's ready. Let's adjourn to the dining room." Well, that was the end of that conversation for the time being, but that sensation of having missed something was gone. I smiled to myself.

Maybe we were getting somewhere after all.

CHAPTER 8

After dinner last night—where we all watched Liv push her favourite meal of roast pork with crackling around her plate and eat hardly any of it—I suggested we carry out a test to prove I could tell the difference between people's magic. Thus, I was in Angelica's living room, standing at the door to the hall, facing out. My eyes were shut under the blindfold Angelica insisted I wear. Will, Beren, Imani, Angelica, James, and Millicent were in attendance. It would be too much of a luck thing if there had only been two people for me to choose from.

My scalp tingled as someone conjured a small spell. "Angelica." Yep, definitely bossy and impatient. No one said anything. They weren't going to tell me until the end how many I got right. The hairs on the back of my neck rose, and a pleasant shiver cascaded down my body. I grinned. "Will." I'd know his magic anywhere. It had more of an effect on me than anyone else's. Clean, honest, and strong power skimmed over my scalp. "James."

We continued for another ten minutes before Angelica finally said, "Okay. We're done."

The blindfold disappeared, and I turned. Will was grinning like he was proud. Angelica and James regarded me with poker faces, before James's broke and he smiled and nodded. Millicent, Beren, and Imani looked at me as if I'd grown a second head, but in an awed kind of way. Will stood and came to me. He wrapped strong arms around me. "You are amazing, but I knew that."

I grinned up at him. "Thank you. It's nice to be appreciated."

"Well, dear, you got them all correct." Angelica raised her brow.

I dropped my arms from around Will. "Don't you believe me? Do you think I cheated?" I put my hands on my hips, ready to defend my honour as my cheeks heated.

"Knowing you, I don't really think you cheated, but…" Her expression softened, and she allowed perplexion to show through.

"But what?"

She shifted her gaze to Will. "You two can talk to each other mind to mind. Maybe there was some of that going on?"

He folded his arms. Angelica was great at offending people because she just didn't care. She was going to air her thoughts no matter what. I sighed. She didn't mean it personally—it was just her. "We can, but we haven't been.

In fact"—he turned to me—"we agreed not to unless it was an emergency. We have phones for that, and if anyone finds out what we can do, we've lost any advantage we might have in the future." By *anyone*, he meant Dana and her group. Will had also explained to me that there was a possibility our mind-to-mind conversations could possibly be listened into, just like a normal phone conversation, and it was a lot of effort to shield them, so we just didn't bother.

"Right. Well, I want both of you blindfolded for the next bit." I rolled my eyes. Not again. Why couldn't they just believe me? "Both of you, turn around."

Will and I gave each other "the things we have to put up with" looks and turned. A blindfold appeared on my face, and I waited. Magic ruffled the hairs on my neck. Gentle, kind, but with an undercurrent of nervousness. "Millicent." We continued for another five minutes.

"Okay, dear." The blindfold disappeared. I turned to face Angelica. "I'm satisfied you have the talent to tell one person's magic from another. You're racking up those talents. I've never seen anything quite like it. Are you *sure* you won't come and work for us?"

"I practically work for you anyway, but no, I don't want a full-time job as an agent. Once we get to the bottom of what happened to my parents, I'm taking a massive holiday. I've always wanted to travel around Europe and take photos. And I'm here for you when you're desperate. Plus, Mill and James are surely going to need some babysitting soon." I grinned at my brother, who returned it. "Sorry." Guilt stomped one of those stiff yet vigorous Irish dances in my stomach, but it wasn't enough to get me to change my mind. The stress of the last few months had been ridiculous. I couldn't imagine what doing that job for a lifetime would do to me. I didn't want to be in danger if I didn't have to, and once the stupid snake group was taken care of, I would be able to live my life in peace. I was really, really, really looking forward to that day. The money they paid me as a "consultant" was great, but if I picked up more photography work, I'd easily make a living out of it.

"I'd like to check in on Liv before I go to work. Can you update me on what we're doing about this later?" Beren stood and ran a hand through his hair. I was planning on dropping in on her later too. We'd decided to tag team as much as we could because Liv wasn't doing too well. I was going to pass by Costa and grab some supplies first.

"Of course, dear. James will let you know. I'll see you later." Angelica gave her nephew a nod, and he made his doorway and left. She turned back to us. "So, at this stage, we can assume with reasonable confidence that Lily has singled out Owen the Oracle as a potential suspect in these unusual incidents. Unfortunately, that doesn't give us enough of a reason to demand a list of his clients so we can follow up what's been happening in their lives, or the lives of those closest to them. Any suggestions on motive?"

"Maybe he hates non-witches?" I shrugged. As far as we could tell, none of the victims of the unusualness had been witches. "Unless that spell he's using doesn't work on witches?"

"Could be." Millicent, reclined in one of the Chesterfields, rubbed her belly. "But why would he do something to hurt his clientele? They're the reason he has so much money and success. Maybe he's linked to Regula Pythonissam somehow?"

I'd considered that. They were always looking at ways of causing trouble, and they did hate non-witches… at least, that's what we assumed. "Maybe he takes money to do stuff to people? Like, his fortune telling is a front for other services for hire?"

Will shook his head. "I don't think so. Besides, he'd be leaving himself too open to arrest—letting non-witches know he was a witch and could arrange for things to happen to people?"

"He might just put himself out there as being a normal person who can get the job done, like an assassin." I was clutching at straws, but brainstorming was like that—you had to crack a few eggs to make a cake, or was that an omelette? I much preferred cake…. In any case, I wasn't afraid of being laughed at for stupid ideas—goodness knew I did enough stupid stuff on a regular basis to worry about that now.

Angelica sat next to Millicent and smoothed her black knee-length skirt once she was comfortable. "Anything is possible. To that end, we have those interviews with the victims of the other incidents underway, but I'd like to set up… not quite a sting, but a chance to find out more." She held her hand up, and small pieces of paper appeared in it. "These are tickets to Owen's next show in London. It's happening tonight. I'm sending Lily, James, Will, and Gus."

Huh? "Gus? As in, Gus the security guy?" Gus the guy who always managed to gross me out with his ew-filled conversations.

She nodded. "He was rather excited to be included. Since he's a non-witch, he's perfect for what we need. I've gotten him one of the few spots to have a reading after the show. He'll be wired. I want you there, Lily, to make sure when Owen casts any spells, you can get another feel of his magic, reconfirm that's the one we're looking for. James and Will are going to be there to see who else is having readings. We're going to keep an eye on all those people, tail them, see what happens in their lives. We'll also be listening in on all the readings."

My mouth dropped open. "That can't be legal. What if none of those people are actually in on whatever he's doing, assuming he is the one doing it, and it isn't all just a huge coincidence? What about people's privacy? Kate's friend could have set Liv up. Are you tailing her?"

"In the interests of crime solving, it's legal. We can pretty much do whatever we want if we feel we have reason. Now, I suggest you prepare for tonight. You'll be leaving at 6:30 p.m. If Owen happens to see you, tell him you enjoyed his reading so much the other night that you just had to come."

Grrr, she'd ignored my question about Kate. "I don't know about that. I… um, kind of had an altercation with him at a flower shop. He knows I don't like him."

Her brows raised, then slammed down as she frowned.

"What kind of altercation, dear?" Her voice was calm, too calm.

"I just ranted at him a teeny bit." I blew out a loud breath. "Well, he didn't warn Liv about what would happen. If he's such a good freaking fortune teller, why couldn't he have warned her? And if what he does is all for show, how dare he mess with people like that? Get their hopes up. What if someone believes the thing they want most is going to happen and they wait a lifetime, always saying no to things that could have been good, only to die without getting what they wanted?" I folded my arms and thumped them onto my chest.

"Well, wear a wig or something. Make sure you're unrecognisable. Will was at that party too, wasn't he?"

"Yes," he answered. "I'll grow a beard. Lily and I will stay at a distance. He won't notice us. And James—well, he wasn't at Liv's party, so if there's anything we need to do close up, we'll get him to do it. He can accompany Gus to his reading and wait outside the tent, or room, or whatever he's going to use."

"Good. We're settled on it then." Angelica stood. "Gus will be wired, and to make sure Owen can't read all of his thoughts, we've blocked all PIB memories. If he tries to access those, it will trigger run-of-the-mill security-guard ones. Gus's cover is that he works security for a bank. We've already implanted the false memories, and Gus has *experienced* them, so to speak. So we're good to go."

"Why couldn't you just do that with Will's memories

when he went undercover?" It surely would've made things less risky with Piranha.

Will shook his head. "It takes power to create those memories. If you put them in too strongly, you could end up embedding them permanently and erasing the other memories. Anything in someone's brain must be handled with extreme care. These memories will fade after a couple of days, and the block will fade from his other memories. He can still access some of the real memories, of course, but that's only because the block is gentle enough that it will fade after forty-eight hours."

"Right." This stuff was complicated. At least for me. I was sure I'd be much happier if I just stopped asking questions.

Will smiled. "Don't worry about that stuff, Lily. That's what we're for. Just worry about what you need to do."

"Okay, boss." I saluted.

Angelica cleared her throat and gave me an "I beg your pardon" look. I grinned and shrugged. "Well, technically, he's my boss on this case. He answers to James, who answers to you, and Will's my direct report."

"Hmm, so you're going to do what I say?" There was a distinctly mischievous twinkle shining from his eyes.

"Maybe...." I laughed. "I'll do my best."

He growled, which was kind of sexy, although I was sure he didn't mean it to be. "I've heard that before."

"Okay, kids, enough. We have to get going." James stood and took Millicent's hand. We've got work to do." He looked at Will. "I'll meet you at my place. We'll take my car to the next interview." He looked back at me. "After Will gets you tonight, we're going to travel to nearby toilets. And make sure your mind-shield is up."

"Yes, dear. You're on the job tonight. Do what you're told and be careful."

I sighed. Seriously, when were they going to stop treating me like I was ten? "I'll be careful."

Angelica raised one sceptical brow. "Lily...." The warning in her voice was clear.

I crossed the fingers of one hand, which she couldn't see because they were covered by my folded arms. "And I'll only do what I'm told." The heat of everyone's gazes was on me. It was like being at an Aussie beach in the middle of the day in the middle of summer—scorching and uncomfortable. I squinted and resisted the urge to put a shielding hand above my eyes—if only I had a large umbrella to hide behind. "I know you have lots of work to do, so I'll see you all later. Have fun." I grinned.

James shook his head, and Millicent smirked. Angelica's brow was still high, shining its displeasure down on me. Will gave me a quick kiss on the mouth. "See you later, trouble-maker." Hmm, catchy. I liked it.

I waved as they all departed through magical doorways. Which left Imani and me sitting next to each other. She looked at me. "I'll come with you to Costa and then to see Liv. I have to get back to work in a couple of hours, but I'm yours until then." She grinned. As strong as my magic was, I was still under her added protection whenever I went out. Which, to be honest, made me feel safer. Too many things had happened for me to think I could look after myself against the snake group, and after what happened at Millicent's....

"We'd best get going then." I stood. "We can take Angelica's car." Imani had travelled here, and since Angelica had travelled back to the PIB, her car was the answer.

After gathering supplies at Costa, we hurried to Liv's parents'—I wished she could come back home to us, but that wasn't an option until she was cleared of the crime she didn't commit. Her mum let us in and directed us to Liv's childhood bedroom.

"Isn't Beren here?" I asked. I did *not* want to walk in on anything.

"He just left. He had to go to work, so it was a quick visit. He's coming back for dinner."

Okay, so the coast was clear. I still knocked before entering. A muffled and dejected "come in" was the response. Inside, Liv lay in bed, on top of the covers. She was in her favourite cat pyjamas, which had a big cat face on the front that said, "I'd spend all nine lives with you." Her real cat, Eric, a black-and-white tabby, snuggled against her tummy. Liv's hair was a knotted mess, and her eyes were red and puffy. But that wasn't the worst of it.

"Hey." I handed the tray of coffees to Imani and sat on Liv's bed, careful not to scare Eric, and gave her a gentle hug. Yes, hugging wasn't my thing, but she clearly needed it, and that was one thing I could do. When I'd finished, I stood and made space for Imani to administer her hug. She handed me the coffees and the bag of muffins, then tended to Liv.

While she did that, I debated whether to bring up my concerns or not. Sometimes hassling people about a clear problem only stressed them out more. But I needn't have worried—Imani was on the case.

Imani pinched Liv's hip. "Are you fading away on us? Luckily, we brought supplies." She nodded to the food in my hands. "Now sit up. You're going to eat a double-chocolate muffin. And we won't take no for an answer." She stood and put her hands on her hips, waiting for Liv to resettle in a sitting position.

Liv slowly complied, and Eric decided it was his cue to leave. I stared at the door long after he'd left. What if he was the only thing keeping her comforted? I looked back at Liv. "Do you want me to get Eric to come back?"

She shook her head, or rather, moved it slightly from side to side, as if anything more would require too much effort. "When was the last time you ate?" I asked.

She shrugged. Imani and I looked at each other—my worry reflected in her concerned gaze. "Here." I handed Liv a tea and muffin.

"Thanks, but this will make a mess. I'll eat them later." She turned to put them on her bedside table.

I shook my head. "Nope. You'll eat it now. We can"—I waved my hand—"any crumbs away before we leave."

"I'm not hungry." Her voice was so quiet that I almost couldn't hear. Grr, if Kate wasn't already dead, I'd kill her myself. Her and her stupid digs at Liv's weight, and now

Liv's whole life was on a knife edge because of her and her evil friend.

"Sorry, Liv, but we don't care if you're not hungry. You need to eat. You're wasting away. At this rate, you'll disappear by next week." Imani's firm tone was not one you disobeyed easily.

"I ate last night. Honest. Ask my mother if you don't believe me."

"I'll be back." I turned to leave.

A loud sigh came from Liv. "All right. I just want you both to know: I hate you right now. Why can't you just leave me and my depression in peace? Surely I have a right to dwell. My life has just gone down the toilet—a dirty, smelly prison toilet."

"I know how that feels. Before I met you, I was chucked in the PIB prison. I'm sure I've told you the story." She looked at me like "so what?" "You'll need your strength to deal with this. Plus, we're going to get the charges dropped. You didn't do anything wrong. Please just trust us."

"And tell me, Lily—did you feel like eating while you were locked up?" Some heat had returned to her voice. Even though it was anger directed at me, it was better than nothing. I bit down on my smile. We needed to get her fired up enough to fight this with us.

"No, but that was just because the cell smelt really terrible. At least you're not next to a toilet right now. I'd take full advantage if I were you." I unleashed a fraction of my smile to soften my words. In the mood she was in, she was liable to miss that I was trying to cheer her up.

She scrunched her nose. "Okay, okay. Will you promise to get off my case if I eat this now?"

Imani and I nodded. Liv took a sip of her tea. That was a start—the tea had milk and one sugar in it, but it couldn't compare to the calories in that muffin. I pretty much held my breath until she finally took a bite. Thank God. Imani and I ate our own muffins and chatted about silly, inconsequential things to distract her as she ate. Eventually, it was all gone.

Liv's mum knocked on the door frame. "Hey, girls. Does anyone want anything?"

I turned and smiled. "No thanks. We've all just had our muffins from Costa."

Her mum's eyes widened slightly. "Oh, what kind did you have, Liv?" That must have been her way of asking, without being obvious, if Liv had one too. I guess "we" could have been just Imani and me.

"Same as them. Double chocolate." She looked at us, the tension around her eyes less than what it had been when we'd arrived. "Thanks. It was nice of you to bring me one."

Her mother's smile was huge. "Yes, it was. Thank you. I'll leave you to it." She sent us a look of pure gratitude, then left.

"So," I said, hoping I wasn't about to push her too far. "You're allowed to leave the house, aren't you?"

She shrugged. "Yes, but I don't want to."

"Not even to visit Angelica's? Maybe you could come hang out tomorrow?"

She scratched her arm. "I have to go the station tomorrow, to check in, you know, for my bail conditions." She blushed.

"Stop. Just stop," said Imani. Huh? I stared at her. "Liv, none of this is your fault, for goodness' sake. There's nothing to be ashamed of. The police should be ashamed, and so should that cow who lied about you knowing Kate was going to be at the movies. Don't be despondent—be angry. Act like the innocent person you are. Don't let them beat you. They're going to be apologising before too long. I promise. And Kate's friend will get arrested for lying. Hopefully, I'll be the one who gets to make the arrest."

Liv's expression was thoughtful. "I'm sure Beren would like to join you." Atta girl! She was gradually getting on board.

I smiled. "I'd like to get in a couple of sneaky punches before the arrest, to be honest."

Liv's lips twitched. "Promise I can be there to watch?"

"Definitely." Okay, so I shouldn't be condoning violence, but if that's what it took to cheer her up, I was all for it.

All too soon, it was time to go. I magicked the crumbs off her bed. "Done."

"Thanks… for everything." Liv stood, and I smiled. Yay, she was out of bed!

I gave her a hug. "Sorry we have to go, but Imani has to get to work, and I can't be out on my own." Looked as if Liv wasn't the only one with a prison sentence. To be fair, her situation was much worse, but still, Dana's snake group had way too much to pay for. "Honestly, see if you can come over tomorrow. If you can't, I'll pop over at some point—either with Imani or Will."

Liv nodded way more vigorously than her head shaking earlier. "Okay. You girls are amazing, you know that?"

"We do, actually, but it doesn't hurt to hear someone else say it." Imani grinned and gave her a hug. "See you soon, love."

As we left, as much as Liv had seemed better than when we'd arrived, something else bothered me, and yet again, I couldn't decipher what it was. Unfortunately, I had a feeling it was important.

CHAPTER 9

The bright spotlight shone on the black-caped Owen the Oracle and the latest guinea pig on stage with him. The twenty-something-year-old woman with long, straight brown hair—his ninth guest—sat in a chair. Owen stood next to her. They both faced the crowd. Owen had one hand on her head and his eyes shut. His other hand rested on his crystal ball, which sat on a table next to him, swirling grey and white, as if it were a portal that was about to spew a storm into the room.

His magic shuddered over my scalp. I shut my eyes, breathed in, and gave over to the sensation of it. A strong thrum of hope, overlaid with an equal amount of arrogance and a suggestive hint of… chaos? Move over, wine connoisseurs; here comes your magic equivalent. I smiled, even though this was serious. The image of me swirling the golden magic from the river in a wine glass came to me.

Imagination-me sniffed it and took a sip. Hmm… a hint of berries. If only it was harmless. Which also led me to wonder if magic could be drunk, as in someone could drink it, not drunk. Drunk magic was bad, or performing magic drunk was. I remembered the night at Marcia's birthday when one of her older granddaughters was performing fire magic under the influence. It could've ended very badly. *Anyway, Lily, brain back on the job, please.*

Could I imbibe other people's magic if I tried? I could give it away, so I guessed I should be able to receive it. Not that I wanted anyone else's—mine was enough of a pain to deal with.

"Is he using magic?" the grey-haired, long-bearded man sitting next to me asked in a quiet voice.

I grinned. "Yes, Grandpa. And it's exactly what I thought it was."

He nodded, then cocked his head to the side. "Is that a hair growing out of your chin?" He leaned close to me in the darkened theatre.

"Very funny." I narrowed my eyes, pushed my glasses up my nose, and smoothed the fabric of my elastic-waisted orange trousers over my thighs. Dressing up as a couple of oldies had been my idea. I even had stick-on wrinkles and a cane. Will's grey-blue eyes were still as heart-stopping as usual, even behind all that distinguished hair. In a whisper, so as not to disturb those around us, I said, "Now, shhhh. I'm trying to watch the show."

We sat about midway between the stage and back wall in the large theatre, while James and Gus sat two rows from the front. They had the special seats since *Gus* had paid extra to have his fortune read afterwards. Only a select few were having it read in front of the crowd. And that made our job a hell of a lot easier. I'd turned my phone on to record video of everything at the beginning of the show. I'd put a no-notice spell on myself before I entered so I could hold it up without anyone telling me not to. The sign at the entry door said no recording devices. I smirked, enjoying my little foray into naughty territory. *Ooh, Lily, such a rebel.* I laughed at myself. Okay, so I was a decent person—sue me.

He finished with the woman on the stage, swirling his cape with one arm as he gestured to her with the other. "Please thank Vera, everyone." The crowd dutifully clapped. "And now I'd like to call Brian Perkins to the stage." I lowered my camera as Owen scanned the audience, watching for Brian to emerge—no-notice spells tended not to work on witches. Only two of his team appeared to be witches, and they were near the front of the stage as security.

As overweight Brian, in a too-tight shirt and jacket, waddled up the stage stairs, I lifted my camera. Crap. My intake of breath must have alerted Will. "What's up?" he whispered.

I tilted the screen his way. He looked at it, then at me, and scrunched his face in confusion. Oh, that's right—I was the only one who could see it as it was happening. Everyone else would have to watch the recordings later, or they'd miss it. I leaned towards him and whispered, "Brian's see-through." Adrenaline swooshed through my chest and stomach in an uncomfortable dip. Will's mouth formed a silent O. His sad face mirrored my feelings. I swivelled back to face the stage.

"So, Brian, are you ready to find out your future?" Anger burned briefly in my chest—what future, Owen, hmm? He definitely wasn't any good if he couldn't see Brian wasn't going to be around much longer.

Brian, sitting facing the crowd, nodded.

Owen held a palm card up, which he looked at before putting in his pocket. "It says here that you want to find out if your dream of selling one of your paintings to a stranger for over two-thousand quid will come true. It also says you want to know if you're ever going to meet the woman of your dreams, and, if so, when." He grinned. "I can help you with that. Are you ready to know your future, Brian?" A few diehards in the audience clapped and cheered.

Brian nodded enthusiastically. His broad smile was full of joy. I gritted my teeth. That poor man. So oblivious. Maybe I should follow him around, or have Beren follow him, revive him if he dies. But then again, we couldn't save everyone. What if it was his time to go for whatever reason? And was it right for Owen not to warn him? I supposed if he said anything, the guy would just be stressed until it happened, which is not the way you want to spend the last few hours or days of your existence. I sighed.

Owen rested one hand on Brian's head and the other on the crystal ball. He shut his eyes, and his magic peppered my scalp. "Hmm… interesting. Ah, yes.…"

Brian sat up straighter, hope in the set of his shoulders.

He looked like a British bulldog who's just been told he's going for a walk.

"I see a painting of a woman in the rain. She holds a red umbrella. Very nice oil painting, Brian. This is the one that will sell, and it will sell for well over two-thousand quid. And it will happen soon. Very soon." He smiled and nodded. "Now, let's see if you'll meet the woman of your dreams."

Many of the people sitting around me, except for Will, leaned forward, waiting to hear the outcome. The tension in the room was almost as palpable as Owen's magic. Did this room full of strangers care about Brian, or was it just that if there was hope for his dreams to come true, there was hope for theirs?

Owen snatched his hand off the ball and opened his eyes. The crystal, which had flashed with bright colours— orange, white, blue, and green—settled back into its swirling white and charcoal grey. "You're going to meet the woman of your dreams even sooner than selling your painting. You'll both be wearing green. Her blonde hair will be in a braid when you first meet." Wow, that was specific. I bet Brian wore green everywhere from now on. How much was this a premonition, and how much of it was suggestively motivated?

Brian's grin suggested he was happy. "I love blondes." He looked up adoringly at Owen.

Owen's return smile was slightly skewed. "Ah, yes, I know." The crowd laughed. "And that, ladies and gentlemen, is our last guest for the night! Please clap your hands for Brian!" As Brian made his way off stage, I stopped recording and put my phone in my bag. Just as I did, it vibrated with an incoming message since the ringer was on silent.

As I took my phone back out of my bag, Owen thanked everyone for coming. "Thanks for the love. Because of you, my fans, I've just been named Fortune Teller of the Year for the UK. There's nothing I love more than sharing news of people's futures, especially when I'm letting them know their dreams are going to come true. That's the best part of my job, for sure. Thank you all for letting me share my gift with you. For anyone who has private readings, please stand now, and my friend Ewan will take you through. Goodnight, everyone, and may the cosmos give you everything you desire!" He waved using his whole arm as if he was trying to get someone's attention. I wanted to tell him it was okay, we could see him, but whatever.

Now the theatrics were over, I looked down at my phone. The message was from Angelica. *Lily, we require your presence at the conference room right now. Imani, Beren, and I are waiting. You are excused from Owen's show. Tell Will he's to stay and cover James. Please answer YES and get here ASAP.*

Yikes, that sounded urgent, but I couldn't resist a smile. It was like when you had a doctor's or hairdressing appointment and they messaged the day before. *Answer YES to confirm your appointment.*

I typed out YES and sent it. I turned to Will. "Ma'am's asked me into the PIB for an urgent meeting with B and Imani. She said you're to stay here." I showed him the message.

His wrinkly brow furrowed, his newly grey brows dipping down, and he searched my eyes. "Do you have any idea what this could be about?"

I shook my head. But then my stomach took a dive. "Maybe it's something to do with Liv. What if she's back in jail, or worse...." Everything she'd been through had depressed her. Maybe she figured it was all too hard. *Please no.* Nausea inched up my throat.

Will gently grabbed my upper arms. "Don't jump to conclusions. It's probably just new information, and Ma'am doesn't have anyone else to cover it. While you're there, you can transfer the video from tonight as well. Text me, and let me know what's up. Okay? And no catastrophising." Under normal circumstances, I would comment on how cute that word was, but in light of what might be happening, my heart wasn't in it.

"I'll do my best. I'll text you." We stood, and he dropped a lingering, close-mouthed kiss on my lips.

"Stay safe. Love you."

"Love you too."

As Will carefully made his way over to watch James and Gus, I did my best to walk slowly, with my cane, to the toilets. It took all my willpower to plant the cane and hobble slowly. Damn being old. And being old was when you wanted to get stuff done because you didn't have long left. Having to go slow was not conducive to getting things done. Like old drivers who went under the speed limit. I always wanted to beep at them and shout, "You don't have long left. Why are you wasting time?" My legs were slow, but my brain was spewing nonsense at two hundred kilometres per hour. Sometimes it sucked to be me. Well, quite often lately.

Eventually, I made it. There was a long line, and, of course, anyone watching me go into the out-of-order cubicle would think I was nuts, or maybe just senile. Although, it could work because even if they saw me go in, they'd be going to the toilet and leaving, so they'd not hang around to see if I ever came out. Also, I had my no-notice spell on, and there was only one witch I could see in here. I'd just have to be careful not to bump into anyone as I limped past —why did the out-of-order cubicle always have to be the one at the very end?

My back prickling with conspicuousness, I entered the cubicle. As soon as the door closed, I made my doorway to the PIB and, giving the old girl the flick, I jumped through.

CHAPTER 10

Okay, so jumping wasn't such a great idea. I sat in the conference room while Beren held a hand over the huge bump on my forehead, readying to heal it. "Honestly, Lily. How did you manage this?"

Heat suffused my cheeks. "It wasn't my fault. Someone rearranged the furniture in the reception room. I crashed into it, tripped, and flew into the wall." Imani snorted from her seat across the table, but I couldn't give her the stink eye since Beren was in front of me.

The warmth of his healing on my bump matched the temperature of my cheeks.

"But how? Walking into a chair shouldn't end up with you flying into the wall at the velocity you'd need to cause this bump." Imani sniggered. Her commentary was not appreciated.

"What's so funny?" I grumbled as Beren removed his hands. I felt my forehead, and the bump was gone. "Thanks, B."

Imani still wore a stupid grin. "I can just see how it happened. I'd bet my favourite pair of Louboutins that you weren't walking when you came through your door. It's just a shame I missed it." The only positive about Imani laughing was that Liv must be okay. I couldn't see Imani being anything but upset if something had happened to our friend.

I gave her my best death glare. At least Ma'am wasn't in the mood either. She folded her arms. "Right, enough of that. We have some serious business to attend to." Beren sat next to me as she continued. "We have some new information, thanks to the interviews we've been conducting. Kate's friend Olga, the one who was at the movies, has been identified as knowing the man who was killed by the tiger."

Olga? She didn't look like an Olga. An Olga, to me, was someone tall and huge, like a tough Russian woman you wouldn't mess with. This woman was slim, long-legged, and gorgeous; also, there was no hint of a Russian accent.

"Lily? Are you listening?" Ma'am pressed her lips together, obviously annoyed.

"Um, yes. Sorry." I looked at her with wide, I'm-paying-super-attention eyes. *Brain, focus, damn you.* "Before we get started, how's Liv?" I looked at Beren.

His concerned expression didn't change. "Not great. A bit better after your visit, and her mother said she's eating a tad more, but she's still depressed and worried. Unfortunately, there's not much we can do. It's a normal reaction to her circumstances, to be honest. The only thing that will really help is for us to solve this disaster."

"Agreed." I turned back to Ma'am. "How did Olga know him?"

She humphed, probably irritated at being interrupted. Hmm, that was two things I'd done so far at this meeting, and we'd only just started. I was in fine form today. "Olga and Irving were acquaintances who met in a Westerham animal-lovers Facebook group. He'd posted that he was going to the park that day, in case anyone wanted to go with them. But a couple of weeks prior to that, he'd posted something about marriage equality on his own wall, which was public, and she attacked him for being gay, said homosexuality was unnatural, plus a few other choice things. He blocked her, but he'd taken screenshots. His partner provided them."

Oh, wow, Olga was even more horrible than I thought. In her world, it was a crime to be fat or gay. Considering how many people were fat or gay, she must have been angry a hell of a lot. Good. I hoped her brain melted from the heat of her anger. "Can you prove she killed him?"

"No. But she visited the animal park the day before. We've got a specialist team combing the grounds for her magic signature. They've also checked out the tiger, to see if she cast a spell on it to attack him."

"Have you tied her to any of the other things we're looking at?" Imani asked.

"Not yet, but we have an agent tailing her."

I sat up straighter. "What if she had something to do with Kate's death? She seems horrible enough to want to kill her friend. Maybe Kate had angered her somehow? She might have just taken the opportunity to kill her with magic after Liv pushed her. Maybe she magicked an invisible thing for her to trip over?"

Imani shook her head. "If that was the case, we would have picked up a strong magic signature on the day. And to be honest, the thing with Liv was random, and Olga wasn't in the room when it happened."

"True, but what if she had a way of spying on Kate and was just waiting for the perfect time to hurt her?" At this point, I was going to clutch at every straw, no matter how dry, brittle, and likely to snap it was. Now that I thought about it, were they supposed to be pieces of straw, or the ones you drank with? Wow, I was pretty dense. I really had no idea. I was going with pieces of straw like cows ate, but maybe I was wrong. I'd have to google it later because there was no way I was asking anyone. Everyone thought I was ditzy enough as it was. No need to give them any more fodder. I smirked at myself. At least my ability to pun was working.

"I have no idea." Angelica tilted her head sideways. "Why are you smiling?"

"Oh, nothing. Private joke." My stupid cheeks warmed again. At this rate, I was going to give myself sunburn, or would I have to call it shameburn?

"I have to say, dear, that your ability to concentrate this

evening is dismal, even for you." Her flinty stare also imparted how disappointing I was.

I swallowed a sigh. "Sorry. Maybe I'm tired from using my magic to record the whole of Owen's show. Oh, that reminds me." I unlocked my phone and handed it to her. "You might want to copy that over."

"Thank you." She whispered something, and a laptop appeared on the table in front of her. She plugged my phone in via a charging cord and transferred the information, then handed the phone back.

"Thanks."

Ma'am looked at each of us. "Why don't we watch this and see if we can decipher anything, figure out what he's doing?"

Gah, I didn't want to watch it again. I wanted to go and check on Liv, but by the way the meeting had gone already, Ma'am wasn't in the mood to argue. I sucked it up. "There isn't really much to decipher. It's pretty straightforward, but I guess it's good to watch so you can get an idea of the people who were there."

She mumbled another spell, and the familiar tingle of her magic danced across my scalp. A huge TV screen descended from the ceiling on the wall behind Ma'am. We all turned to look at it as whatever was on her computer sailed across the ether and played on the screen. I know I said I'd suck it up, but having to watch the whole thing again was torture. I'd already sat through it once. I failed to see what new information I'd pick up. I covered my yawn and wriggled my bottom, trying to find a more comfortable position in my chair.

It was going to be a boring hour and a half. But I should have relished it because it was way better than what was coming. When would I learn?

CHAPTER 11

Last night, I didn't get to see Liv. I called her to find out if she was okay with me turning up so late, and her mother answered her mobile, said she'd eaten dinner and gone to bed early, as she was exhausted. Beren still dropped in to see her parents and look in on her. He texted me when he was done and said Imani and I should turn up around lunchtime. So now we stood on her front porch with her favourite Indian food for lunch—samosas, beef vindaloo, tandoori chicken, and aloo matar.

I knocked. A few seconds later, the door opened. "Liv!" I stepped forward and gave her a hug, then stepped aside so Imani could do the same. "You're answering the door!"

She smiled. "Yeah, progress, right? I'm feeling a bit better today. I went to the station and checked in. They were actually nice about it—one of my friends was on the front desk. She quietly said she can't believe they charged me, and she hopes I get off."

"That's wonderful, but isn't that against police protocol?"

Liv shrugged. "I think so, but that makes it even nicer that she said it. Made me feel a bit better, you know." I was all for her feeling better, so I smiled. "Anyway, come in. It's freezing out here." She looked at the sky. "News said we might even get snow tonight."

My eyes widened. "Oh my God. You better not be teasing me. I've only waited the whole winter to see snow here."

Imani laughed. "Doesn't take much to torture you, does it, love?" I shook my head and headed into the kitchen with the bags of food, the girls following.

When we reached the kitchen, Liv took one of the bags and looked inside. "That smells divine. Oh, wow, you got all my favourites! Thank you!"

I grinned. "Well, we're kind of being selfish too. I love Indian. We got enough for your parents too."

"Oh, that's so nice of you, but they're going out for lunch. They've spent so much time cooped up at home looking after me, and they can see I'm feeling a bit better, plus they knew you were coming over for the afternoon, so I told them to go do something for them. Dad's had time off work to make sure I've been okay, and he's going back next week. I figured it was only fair they get to have some downtime. They've had a terrible time of this too." She frowned.

"I feel so bad for them. I still can't work out how things went downhill so quickly." She sighed.

It was a mess. "Hey, it wasn't your fault. And that's why it's all going to get cleared up soon. The PIB are working around the clock to figure this out."

Imani looked at me as if to say, "Keep your mouth closed about the details." I gave her a small nod. The investigation was confidential, and I didn't want to get her hopes up, or confuse her more. There were two suspects, and I had my money on Olga at this stage. As much as I thought Owen was incompetent, or even uncaring, I didn't think he'd done anything to make the whole thing happen between Liv and Kate.

Olivia got some plates and cutlery out. "Is it okay if we eat now? I'm starving."

Imani and I shared a smile, and we grabbed the containers of food. "For sure." I looked at Liv. "Did you eat breakfast today? And sorry if I sound like a nagging mother, but, you know…."

"I did actually, although I didn't have much because of going to the police station. I had a banana, but on the way back, we stopped at Costa, and I got a cheese and ham croissant. But I'm hungry again. Probably making up for the last week."

Her clothes hung off her, which was weird because it had only been a week, and now that I really looked, her face seemed even thinner than a couple of days ago. "Well, it's about time your appetite returned; otherwise you might just disappear." My laugh was half-hearted. I didn't want to worry her, but I couldn't help asking. "Have you hopped on the scales lately? It looks like you've dropped a couple of dress sizes."

"I haven't, but you're right. These clothes fit me perfectly before. I had to put a belt on these jeans this morning or they'd fall down, and my bras are too big. I'm not worried, though. Now I'm eating again, I'll put it back on, and probably more." She grinned. "As much as Kate made me feel like crap, I'm shrugging it off. I looked great before this whole thing started, and I can't be bothered buying a whole new wardrobe, so operation Get Back to Size Ten is on. Plus, Beren likes curves." She blushed.

"You're so cute." Imani laughed. "Come on then, loves. I'm hungry too. Let's enjoy this lunch."

After lunch, in which Liv had three bowlfuls, and I was taking as a major success, we hung out and watched a movie. Her parents got home at five, and Imani and I said our goodbyes. Imani dropped me home and went to work. When I walked in the door, Will called out, "Lily, is that you?"

"Yes. Where are you?"

"In the kitchen. Want a cap?"

"Yes please." By "cap," he meant cappuccino—it was just too long a word to have to say the whole thing. I was all for shorthand. As I walked into the kitchen, it appeared on the table. "Mmm, lots of chocolate on the top. You're the best." I gave him a kiss.

He grinned. "Only the best for my lady."

"Ooh, smooth." I sat down and took a sip. He sat next to me. "So, what happened after I left last night?"

"Not much. We recorded all the private readings. Gus asked to find out about a promotion at work, which he actually wasn't going for, but we implanted that desire, and he also asked about his cousin, who is actually on the list for a heart transplant. If he doesn't get one in the next six months, he's going to die."

"What the hell? For real?" His sad expression confirmed it. I pouted. "That's terrible. Poor Gus, and his poor cousin. What did Owen say?"

"He said Gus would get a promotion in the next two weeks, and that his cousin would get the heart he needed, but that it might take a couple of months."

I quirked my top lip up on one side. "You have got to be kidding me. How the hell can he say those things and assume they're going to come true?"

Will shrugged. "What that means, though, is that you're going to have to stick close to Gus for the next two weeks, whenever he's at work."

"What?" What the hell was this? I didn't think I could stand two weeks of vomit and poo stories, or haggis ones. "Do I have to stay with him, or can I be within one hundred metres?"

Will chuckled. "Will you be able to detect when Owen's puff of magic goes off from a hundred metres away?"

"I have no idea." I groaned. "I'd say twenty metres to be safe. That means I'm practically going to have to be with him the whole time, running around the PIB and trying not to throw up."

"What?"

"You know, his gross stories. I swear he has no clue. I've never met anyone who can turn any story into a horrible experience."

He patted me on the back. "Don't worry. It's for a good cause, and it could be a good opportunity for you to practice your poker face. It needs a lot of work."

I shook my head. "That is not incentive. I tell you what; I'll practice my poker face and then come home and repeat all the stories and test your poker face. How does that sound?"

He put his hands up in surrender. "That won't be necessary. Besides, why would you want to relive it?"

He made a good point. I folded my arms and scowled. The things I did for my friends. I was blaming Olga and Kate, though. If it weren't for them, none of this would have happened. Why oh why did Liv's mum have to invite them to her party?

And that's how I found myself at the PIB the next morning at 6:00 a.m., eyes half closed. I walked through my doorway carefully, and I managed to avoid crashing into anything. Yay me. I buzzed, and my companion for the next two weeks answered the door. "Miss Lily! Good morning. I hear we'll be spending lots of time together. It'll be nice to have some company. Some days not much happens, and"— he leaned closer and dropped his voice to a conspiratorial whisper—"it can get a tad boring."

Those were a lot of words to be stringing together this early. I blinked while they sunk into my sleepy brain. "Mmm, yes. It'll be fun. Do you mind if I go down and grab a coffee? Have you got time?"

He smiled. "Yes, I sure do. I have this." He pointed to his earpiece. "If anyone wants me, they'll contact me, and if anyone buzzes the reception room, it lets me know."

"Awesome." I'd been here enough times to know where the cafeteria was, so I started off down the hallway, Gus jogging to keep up. I was tired, but I figured if I walked fast enough, maybe he'd be too busy breathing hard to be able to talk.

I was wrong.

"Whatever you do, don't order anything with bacon. I had some yesterday for breakfast, and I had the runs all day. I almost had to go home so I'd be all right for the Owen thing. There was one moment that I almost didn't make it." He huffed a laugh out with his labouring breaths. Would it be weird if I actually started running?

"Mm-hmm. Thanks." That was a double-edged thanks. Partly thanks for the warning, and partly sarcastic thanks for the TMI. Coffee. I needed coffee. I almost cried—I'm not kidding—when the cafeteria door came into view.

As I hurried through, a lady in the same uniform as Gus's looked up from her breakfast and said hi to Gus. "Hi, boss."

"Why don't you stay and chat while I order. Do you want anything?"

"No thanks, Lily, but great idea." He smiled.

Gee, that was easy. I left them to it and ordered a cappuccino and toasted cheese-and-tomato sandwich. I wanted to have a chocolate muffin, but if I waited till later, I'd get to look forward to it. Anticipation was half the fun.

A few minutes later, food in hand, I walked super slowly to Gus—okay, maybe I was overreacting, but honestly, I was going to eat. He looked happy chatting to his boss, so I stopped and sat two tables away. I could still hear what they were saying, but I could zone out, and didn't I deserve to eat breakfast without wanting to throw up?

I swallowed a mouthful of coffee, then bit into the warm yumminess of my sandwich. Mm, I guessed I could get used to this, and it was only two weeks.

I stopped mid-chew. My eyes widened. There it was, the tingle of magic I'd been sent here to detect. I looked around.

Gus was talking, and his voice caught my attention. "Moira, are you all right?"

His boss was jerking her chin up, hacking, and frantically waving one arm. I jumped up and ran over. "Gus, she's choking!" My heart raced. What was I supposed to do? Stick my finger down her throat and grab the food, or should I try that Heimlich manoeuvre? Hang on. I was a witch—obviously a not-very-smart one, but still. I drew into my well of power. "Whatever food is stuck in her throat, make it come out now."

She gave an almighty cough that sounded a bit like she was retching, and what I think was bacon flew out and splatted on the table. She dragged in huge, wet-sounding gasps and blinked back tears.

"Are you okay?" I asked.

She took a moment to self-assess; then she looked at me. "Yes. Thank you." A few more quick breaths. "I thought I was going to die. You saved my life. Thank you. A thousand times, thank you."

Gus's face was paler than usual. "Are you all right, Gus?"

He nodded. "Yes. Thank you, Lily. You saved Moira's life." He swallowed, his Adam's apple bobbing. His haunted gaze met mine. "Can we have a chat?"

This time, I was pretty sure I knew what he was going to say, and it wasn't about his dog or bowel movements. "Yes, Gus. Come on." I looked at his boss. "Are you okay? Do you want to go to the sickbay or something?" I had no idea if they even had one. I guess we weren't at school. They probably just sent people home if they weren't well.

"I think I will go and get checked out. Do you know if Beren's in?"

I shrugged. "I have no idea."

"It's okay. I'll go to the infirmary. If Beren's not around, Dr Evans is good. He's a witch, but he's studied at medical school—he's a certified doctor."

"Okay, we'll come with you." I grabbed my barely eaten breakfast—I could eat it when I chatted with Gus. We dropped her at the infirmary and kept going. "Why don't we do this in Ma'am's office?"

"Okay."

I had no idea if she'd be there, so I texted her. Thankfully, she was and said to come straight up. Gus might have questionable conversational skills, but he was a nice person. He knocked on and opened Ma'am's door for me and followed me in. Ma'am called out from her inner office, "Come on through."

We sat in the guest chairs in front of her desk. Gus fidgeted with his tie, but at least some of his colour had returned. Ma'am observed us before turning to me. "So, what just happened?"

"We were in the cafeteria. I was having breakfast, and Gus was chatting to Moira, his boss. I felt that small burst of Owen's magic, and then Moira started choking. She was going to die, but I managed to spell the food out of her throat. She's in the infirmary getting checked out." Did this mean Olga was off the hook for what happened with Liv because there'd been a definite burst of magic that night, and I'm pretty sure it felt like Owen's? Although I couldn't be 100 percent sure, as I hadn't been paying full attention. That magic pulse had taken me by surprise, but I doubted Olga had the skill to be so subtle. Apparently it was rare.

Ma'am steepled her fingers. "Gus, please look at me." He slowly lifted his head to meet her eyes. "You know this isn't your fault. We asked you to participate in our… experiment, and you have no idea how helpful it's been."

Sweat beaded on his forehead and dripped down his nose. "But… but is that it? Or might it happen again? I mean, the only way I'd get a promotion is if Moira or Henry couldn't work here anymore, and we just saw how

Owen gets obstacles out of the way. I don't want to be responsible for that." He shook his head so hard that droplets of his sweat flung across and splatted on my face. The world stopped turning for a second—I was sure of it. It took a moment for me to breathe again. Why me? What had I done to deserve this? I swiped my sleeve across my cheek and nose and shuddered. I was so going to wash my face as soon as this meeting was over.

Ma'am flicked her curious gaze to me before turning back to Gus. "I'm afraid I don't know if it'll happen again. But we'll keep Lily with you until the time is up, just to make sure. At least she'll be there to stop anything from happening. Won't you, dear?" Her ironclad smile assured me that I would indeed be there to save the day.

"Ah, yes. Of course." I turned to Gus. The poor thing. I should go easier on him. Goodness knew I'd experienced the pain of killing people, even if it was just a matter of wrong place, wrong time. "I'll make sure no one dies. Okay? And what Ma'am said—none of this is your doing. Just like Liv isn't at fault for what happened to Kate. That's why we need to do this. You don't want to see Liv locked in jail for the next ten years, do you?" I hadn't meant to make this a guilt trip. Oops.

His eyes opened wide. "Of course not! Miss Olivia is such a lovely lady. She's the last person who should be in jail. You're right, Miss Lily. This is for a good cause. I'm just not used to being in the middle of things, you know?"

I gave him a gentle smile. "I know, Gus. But you're doing a wonderful thing here. Thank you for helping us."

He returned my smile and gave a nod. "Right. I suppose I best get back to work." He stood and tipped his cap to Ma'am. "Thank you, Ma'am."

I said goodbye to Ma'am, and as we walked out of her office, I excused myself to go to the bathroom. "Can you just mind my stuff?"

"Of course!" He took my coffee cup and paper bag with the sandwich. I hurried into the bathroom and washed my face. Okay, that was two crises averted this morning. *Please, Universe, can we get through the day with no more nasty surprises?* His shift finished at three, and I was counting down the minutes. It was going to be a loooooong day.

***

THE GOOD THING ABOUT TRAVELLING—I LEFT THE PIB AT three, and I was home by 3:02. I walked into the hallway and locked the reception-room door behind me. So much quiet. My shoulders sagged. I missed Liv being here, and even though Will had moved in—apparently he was staying for a while—he wasn't home much. Like Angelica, he worked long hours. And Imani was busy, so I couldn't grab her and visit Liv either. Which meant I couldn't even go for a run. I wasn't in the mood to be alone with my thoughts, but it looked like I would anyway, at least until Will and Angelica got home for dinner.

I might as well make good use of my time. I magicked

my laptop to myself and took it into the sitting room. Outside, the afternoon light was fading into a bruised sky. I shivered—the fireplace was cold and full of ash. I delved into the river of power, pointed at the fireplace, and pictured the woodpile in the shed. "Two logs, please, and kindling." When they appeared in the fireplace, I couldn't help but grin. I'd come a long way since April, arriving here with no idea. I still had a way to go, but I was pretty happy with how much I'd learned in that time, even though some of the lessons had come with a high price. "Ignite." I clicked my fingers for fun—it totally wasn't necessary, but why not add a bit of flounce?

Orange flames popped up in the kindling and licked around the logs. I sat in one of the armchairs next to the fireplace and got to work googling Owen the Oracle. *Who are you, and what is your endgame?* After today, I was pretty sure Olga was just a cow and not actually the cause of our worst problems. Unless she was working with Owen? Nah, she was just a rogue witch, but then, what about the guy and the tiger? Or what if, somehow, she knew what he was doing and had worked out how to emulate it? That would be too much of a coincidence, surely. I took a deep breath before my thoughts raced too far ahead. *One thing at a time, Lily.*

I typed in Owen the Oracle, and a whole heap of listings came up, from articles to websites of the places he'd appeared, and his own website. There were also chat rooms full of people who were fans and talking about their experiences. Hmm, interesting. I started with an article from two years ago from a local Westerham news site—*Owen the Oracle Predicts Bright Future.*

Local flamboyant fortune teller Owen the Oracle has just landed the gig of his career. He's appearing in Germany at an annual fortune-telling extravaganza that attracts the best in the world. He'll be appearing alongside famous names, such as Ellen the Enlightened, Madame Stargazer, and Manfred the Visionary. Owen says, "I've worked hard to get here. I have the best reputation in the business for being the most accurate. I love what I do. I enjoy predicting the good things that are coming up in peoples' lives. It's satisfying. I've always wanted to be the best, and I feel like my time is now." He winks at me. "Actually, I know my time is now. I'm the best in the world, and the word is finally getting out there." We wish Owen the Oracle luck. If you want to see him amaze with his accurate predictions, tune into BBC One Friday night at eight.

I read a couple more articles that were basically him bragging about being the best in the world. A fourth article with one of his contemporaries, reported after an on-air blow-up, was rather eye-opening. Madame Stargazer and Owen were both on the same talk show. Owen the Oracle was arrogant and disrespectful to Madame Stargazer, basically called her a fake, and reiterated that he was the only real deal out there. He even bragged about earning more than anyone else in the business and having the largest fan base. Looked like his motivation for doing what he was doing was fame and ego. Which made sense, as he never told anyone about the bad stuff that was coming up. He wanted to only be the bearer of good news. But where did that burst of magic come in, and why? Was he a sadist at heart? Hmm. Time to read what was in the chat rooms.

I had to sign up to read the comments, but I put in my junk email address and a fake name. I'd likely get some spammy emails because of signing up—I didn't trust any sites with my information. They all sold it, and then my legitimate emails were lost amongst the crap. So it was one email I gave friends and work acquaintances and one for stupid websites. But I digress….

Hmm, these were interesting. And what would make this scenario even better? Another cup of coffee. I magicked one up. It appeared on the table next to my chair. I took a sip and admired the cheery fire flickering in the fireplace. Wow, I was witching like a champion this afternoon. It was nice to find something positive about the day, and I guessed saving Moira this morning was another plus—it was just depressing that she'd needed saving. Stupid bad witches making trouble.

I settled back in the chair and clicked into the first forum.

Percival127—Owen's the real deal. A few weeks after he read my fortune, it all came true. My girlfriend got back with me when she realised the guy she left me for cheated on her, and my grandma, who was sick, got better, and they said she was going to die.

KittyKat—Nice! Two months after I had my reading with him, my dreams came true, and I landed the job I wanted at the local bakery. He said I'd meet the love of my life there too, and I did! We're getting married next month.

SandyMack—I wanted to see him, but at two-thousand quid, I can't afford it. Does he do any free work?

KittyKat—I don't think so. But, honestly, he's worth it. My friend saw him too, and the stuff he said all came true. He really is incredible.

FrankieDogLover—He was good, and the stuff he told me came true, but some bad stuff happened that he never told me.

KittyKat—Like what?

FrankieDogLover—I was having trouble paying my mortgage, and I desperately needed to pick up more shifts at work, but there were none. The week after I saw him, one of the guys from work had a stroke, and another one had a bad car accident. I got more shifts, but, yeah. So I felt bad, like it was my fault.

KittyKat—Sounds like a massive coincidence. Although my friend got her wish of going on a two-month cruise because her gran died and left her some money. But I think that's just the timing. Life is never always good. And how is Owen to know about all the bad stuff that will happen to other people? We're only asking about ourselves, remember.

FrankieDogLover—Yeah, but I still felt bad. He was accurate in his predictions though.

Right, okay. Those could have been coincidences, but from what I could see, good seemed to follow bad in a lot of these scenarios. Was it because the good things couldn't happen without the bad? I mean, everyone had to die, so maybe the granny thing was just luck of the draw, and you could argue the guys at Frankie's work suffered the same bad luck. A lot of people had strokes and car accidents. It didn't prove anything.

I read another forum, and another. They were a mix of the same—he was accurate, but there were always a couple of people who mentioned the balance of good news and the bad that facilitated it. There was something there—I was sure of it. But what, why, and how to prove it, if it was, indeed, intentional on Owen's part.

I stared into the fire and pondered. My phone rang, and I jumped, slamming my hand over my heart. Seriously. I needed to meditate or something. I slid it out of my pocket and answered it. "Angelica. What's up? Is everything okay?" I had the sinking feeling maybe something had happened to Moira again.

"Yes, dear. Things are just fine. I'm calling to tell you that we've arrested Olga."

I sucked in a breath. "What happened? Why? Did she set Liv up?" My heart was racing, and not just because of me being highly strung. Did this mean Liv was off the hook?

"Not that we can tell, but we have untangled a few things with the Irving tiger case. It appears as if Olga was there that morning too. We went over all the surveillance videos. She was wearing a disguise. She must have been there the day before to prepare. After seeing the surveillance video, we called her in and took her magic signature. It matched the faint trace we found at the park that day. She'd done her best to scramble it afterwards, but it was there."

"But what about the burst of magic Alfred, the guy's partner, felt? It's so similar to the Owen things. Can you be sure?"

"At this stage, it's what we have, Lily. I'm not going to go looking for trouble. Now we just have to figure out how to prove she had a hand in what happened to Olivia… if she did. But anyway, I just thought you'd like to know."

"Thanks. So, are you still investigating Owen?"

"Of course, dear, especially after what happened today. Anyway, I'll be home at seven with Will, and we'll have dinner."

"Okay. See you then. Bye." Had anyone told Liv what had happened? Although maybe she shouldn't know. If she got her hopes up and Olga didn't have anything to do with it, it might start another downward spiral. I sighed, my heart heavy. We were getting there, but there was still much to untangle. Thankfully, though, we had time. Liv's trial wasn't for another few months, which was a long time to carry the stress around, but it gave us plenty of opportunity to get to the bottom of what was going on.

At least that's what I thought. As usual, the universe had other ideas.

CHAPTER 12

The next day at eleven, I was preparing to visit Olivia. Rain pelted down outside. Angelica had even set the fire before going to work—it was that cold, but not enough to snow. Rugged up in my black coat, I frowned as I gazed out the window. Christmas was approaching, and I really, really wanted to see it snow by then. If we weren't caught up in everything right now, I'd magic over to Germany or somewhere with plenty of snow. Maybe we'd get Liv off by then, and Will would come with me for a weekend. Dreams are free, as they say.

Imani's car pulled into the driveway. She jumped out and ran to the front door, which I reached at the same time. I yanked it open. Her normally calm composure had slipped. Tension splayed small lines at the corners of her eyes, and her eyes radiated worry. She stood there, mouth poised to say something that wasn't actually coming out. My stomach dropped to the floor. Whatever this was, it wasn't going to be good.

"Are you okay? Imani? Come in." I grabbed her arm, pulled her inside, and shut the door. "What wrong?"

"It's Liv."

Adrenaline released, warming my face and ramping up my heart rate. I was afraid to ask, but.... "What? What happened? She's not d—"

"No! No, she's alive."

I took a deep, shuddering breath. "What then?"

"She's sick. She collapsed this morning, and her parents called an ambulance. She's in the A&E. Beren's with her. The doctors have no idea what's going on. Beren told me to come get you and take you to the hospital. Hopefully he'll have more to tell us when we get there."

"When you say collapsed, is she still unconscious, or is she awake?"

Short, sharp shakes of her head. "I don't know."

"Okay. Let's go."

The drive to East Surrey Hospital took thirty minutes in the downpour. It was the longest thirty minutes of my life. My leg jiggled the whole way, and neither of us said a word. The crappy visibility didn't help as fat droplets pummelled the windscreen. Imani drove slower than normal, leaning forward, her hands clenched on the steering wheel. Each rapid *thunk, thunk, thunk* of the windscreen wipers resonated in my belly. And I'd thought I was tense yesterday. Ha. Another lesson in the fact that things could always be worse.

I bit my fingernails as we reached the hospital and we

found parking. Imani turned off the car and twisted around to grab an umbrella from the back seat. I'd forgotten one in my dash out of the house, but no matter. I dipped into the river, visualised the umbrella in Angelica's closet, called it to me, and it appeared in my hand. If only all our problems were that easily magicked away.

Imani and I shared a glance and a nod; then we bolted from the car to the emergency exit, the pattering rain echoing against my umbrella. At the reception desk, Imani asked if we could go in to see Olivia. The lady behind the desk, petite, olive-skinned, her dark hair short, looked up and over her rectangular glasses. Her forehead bunched, creating a myriad of wrinkles. "And your relation to the patient?"

"We're her best friends."

The woman shook her head. "I'm sorry. It's immediate family and partner only."

I gritted my teeth, about to say something, when I felt a tingle of Imani's power. I'm sure whatever she was doing was probably illegal, but I didn't care. Sometimes rules were meant to be broken. Imani smiled at the woman. "I'm sure you'll understand that we're her very best friends. We're practically related, and she needs us. Can you let us know where to go? We'd really appreciate it." She'd put on a sweet, lilting tone that even had me smiling. Ooh, she was good.

The nurse's stern expression wavered, and she looked at her computer screen again before looking back at Imani.

She bit her lip. "I really shouldn't, you know, but if you really think she needs you…."

"She definitely needs us. And you would be ever so kind to let us see her."

The woman smiled. "Okay. I guess you could call it my good deed for the day." She pointed to double doors. "I'll press the button. Go through, and she should be in a bed there. If she's already been assessed and allocated a room, they'll be able to point you in the right direction."

"Thank you," Imani and I answered. We hurried to the doors, hearing the click of the unlocking mechanism as we reached them.

"Nice work, lady."

"Whatever do you mean?" She grinned and winked.

"Nothing. Nothing at all." I winked back.

Our happiness, however, was short-lived. We were eventually guided to the intensive care unit, where Liv had her own room. Imani stopped in front of the closed door and took a breath. Her gaze met mine. "Ready, love?"

I swallowed. "Not really, but there will never be a good time. Maybe there's something we can do to help." I quirked my lips up on one side as if to say, "You never know."

She opened the door, and we entered.

I tried to keep the shock from my face as I took in the scene. Her parents stood with their backs to us, holding hands, looking down at Olivia, who lay there, eyes closed, heart monitor beeping, a drip in one arm. The room smelt as all hospitals do—disinfectant with the lingering undertone of sickness. And my friend so still. Tears burned, but I blinked them back. Her parents didn't need me coming in here and adding to their grief. It was time to see if there was anything I could do.

"Hey," I said, slowly moving towards the bed.

Her parents turned. Her mother gave us a nod, her father a sad smile. "She's stable," he said. "But they don't know what's wrong. They think it's a metabolic problem."

Beren gave us a chin tip. "They've got more tests to run later." He was on the other side of the bed and held Olivia's hand. The tightness around his eyes spoke of his frustration and pain. I bet he needed to take a good look at what was going on inside, and he couldn't with her parents watching. Right, that was a job I could potentially do, or maybe we needed more of Imani's persuading skills.

"How long have you all been here?" I reached the bed. Liv was so still, her dark skin ashen with a light sheen of sweat on her face. She looked as if she was barely breathing.

Beren answered, "We got here three hours ago. Liv got up, had breakfast, then just… collapsed." He shook his head and gazed down at her.

Her mother sniffed back tears and dabbed her eyes with a tissue. Her father put his arm around her and squeezed her close. I leaned over and touched her cheek. Clammy but hot. "Has she got a fever?"

Beren nodded. "It's come down a bit since they gave her something for it, but she's still burning up." He took a deep breath and blew it out. "They're not doing enough." The fire in his gaze told me we needed to do something *now*. I turned to Imani and gave her a *look*. "I think maybe we should take Mr and Mrs Grosvenor for a little bit of fresh air." I turned to them. "I know you probably don't want to leave right now, but maybe grabbing a cup of tea might help, just take a break, then come back."

Liv's mum shook her head. "I can't leave my baby."

Imani's magic settled over my scalp. "Beren's here with her, and if he needs to, he'll call your mobile. You both need to keep your strength up. She could be here for days. And you don't want to collapse either. It's better for Olivia if you're in good health." Her soothing voice was like a velvety ribbon, swirling around them, drawing them into the idea, lulling them. "If she wakes up while we're gone, Beren will get us straight away. Okay?" Another pulse of magic radiated from her.

Liv's parents both looked at each other, then gave slow nods. "Okay," her dad said. "But only for fifteen minutes. I want to be here if she wakes up."

Imani gave an understanding nod. "Of course. Let's get that cup of tea, and maybe some biscuits. I bet neither of you have eaten yet."

Her mum sniffed back a tear. "Robert and I were about to sit down to breakfast when it happened. I guess we should eat something, even though I feel like I could never eat again." She turned and gazed at Liv.

I patted her shoulder. "I'm sure she'll be better soon. Maybe it's just a terrible virus. But I bet she'll start getting better now she's here. Come on. Let's go and get some sustenance into you both."

Beren gave me a grateful stare and mouthed "thank

you." Imani and I made our way out of the room, Liv's parents reluctantly following. I just hoped whatever was wrong would be fixed by the time we got back. Nausea gripped my stomach. If Beren couldn't help her, nobody could. I blinked back tears. I was not going to cry now. She was still here, if hanging by gossamer. Beren had to be able to fix it.

Imani and I did our best, but the longest we could keep them out of the room was fifteen minutes. I flicked off a text to Beren as we headed back, just to make sure nothing looked unusual when we returned. Her parents were upset enough as it was. We didn't need to freak them out.

I held my breath as we went in, hoping against everything that she'd be awake. But one look at Beren's face freed me from that misapprehension. He gave an almost indecipherable head shake, which was like a punch to the face. He cleared his throat. "Um, I think now you're back, I need to grab a cup of coffee. Lily, Imani, why don't you come with me. I could use the company."

As he walked past Liv's parents, her mother rubbed his arm. He put his hand over hers and gave her a sad smile. "We'll make sure she gets better. I promise." Her forlorn nod brought more tears to my eyes. I turned and headed back to the hallway. *This can't be happening.*

Once we were all outside, we headed back to the cafeteria. Beren made a bubble of silence. "It's a spell I can't untangle. I tried everything. It won't budge. It's like a leech on her energy. It's sped up her metabolism to the point that she can't eat enough to sustain herself, and it's eating through her fat reserves at an alarming rate. Once she's lost those, it will attack her muscles, her heart. She'll die."

I clutched my stomach at the need to throw up. "Who did this to her? Could you tell?"

"Yes." He clamped his jaw for a moment, the muscles bunching. "It's that idiot, Owen the bloody Oracle. I managed to slow it down though, but I couldn't stop it altogether. That's going to buy us a few days at most." He stared straight ahead as we walked, his mouth set in a grim line, jaw ticking. His hands balled into fists that he clenched and unclenched.

"But he'll come and stop it, surely. We need to call him." I mean, that would be the sensible thing to do.

"I already did. I left a message on his answering service just before you guys came back. I didn't mention I was PIB, but I explained what I *assumed* the issue was and asked if he could come and help."

"There's only one problem," Imani said, her voice low. "Once he knows we know what he's done, he may run. I don't know if he meant to do this or why, but if he did, there's no way he'll want to face us."

"But he doesn't know you're the PIB. Maybe it was an accident, a glitch in his future-telling spell?"

Beren turned flinty eyes my way. "I bet it's a side effect of giving people what they want. Don't you see? Liv was upset about being called fat. She must have wished to lose weight or something. Dammit! He gives people what they want. You heard him in that video you recorded." Beren disappeared his spell, whipped out his phone and made a call. "Ma'am, we need to bring Owen in. He's killing Liv." She must have asked how he knew, as he explained what he'd just discovered.

Beren stopped just inside the cafeteria door. He nodded, grunted. "Okay. Fine. Yes. I'll tell them. Bye." He hung up and put the phone in his pocket.

Imani and I both stared at him. He scrubbed a hand through his hair. "I'm staying here with Liv. I'll keep an eye on the spell and see if I can work out how to reverse it or counteract it if I can. Ma'am wants you two in at the PIB. She's agreed to bring Owen in, but even though they've been keeping tabs on him, they can't find him right now. They have to track him down."

My mouth dropped open. "You can't be serious! They knew he was a problem. How could Ma'am let this happen?"

Beren shook his head. "They didn't realise how critical it would be to have him in their sights all the time. They were mainly concentrating on the people he'd seen the other night, tailing them. Honestly, we need more agents. This is ridiculous." He yanked his hair and growled.

"You get back to Liv. We'll come say quick goodbyes, then get going." I grabbed his arm and stared into his sad eyes. "She'll be okay. We'll find him, make him fix this. And you're the best at what you do. I have total faith in you, B." I gave him a quick hug.

"Thanks, but we're not nearly out of the woods. I've never seen anything like it. It's like her body's going to eat itself, and in such a short amount of time. I swear I want to kill every fat-shamer out there, and she was never even fat. Is it cruel of me to say that at least Kate got her comeuppance? This is mostly her fault. What a bloody mess." Mess was an understatement. My best friend lay dying because of cruel people. There was no need for all the hate. What had Liv ever done to them? Sadness lay like lead in my heart.

We hurried back to Liv's room, said goodbye, and left the distraught trio. I gave Liv a kiss on the forehead before we left, scrunching my eyes tight to hold back the tears. It better not be the last time I saw her. If it was, Owen would live to regret it… or maybe he wouldn't… live, that is.

Imani must have seen the murder in my eyes as we left. "Don't do anything stupid, Lily. We need him to disengage his spell."

"I know. I'm just so angry right now. And don't worry: I don't like killing people, and I don't want to go to jail, but a girl can visualise, can't she?"

"As long as that's all you do." She gave me a concerned glance as we opened our umbrellas and ran into the downpour.

I'd rein myself in—I wouldn't do anything to jeopardise Liv's recovery, but the rage searing my insides wanted release. And, for the first time in my life, I was scared… of myself. I'd killed before, more than once, and even though it scarred my soul, was I becoming that person—not an accidental killer, but someone who wanted to exact revenge? Someone who would seek to take another's life?

Imani pressed the beeper on her car. I threw my door open and dropped into my seat, pushing the thoughts away.

I wasn't going to be that person. Nope. My parents would be ashamed. I couldn't let circumstances change who I was. I needed to be better than that. Maybe if I told myself that enough, the worm of unease crawling in my belly would disappear.

I crossed my fingers as I stared into the liquid greyness outside the car. But it wouldn't be enough. Somehow, I needed to find strength before it was too late.

CHAPTER 13

Back at the PIB conference-room table, Ma'am drummed her fingers on its surface. It was like the thrum of tiny racehorse hooves galloping. The cuteness was lost on me today, though. Will sat opposite me —to Ma'am's left—and Imani sat to her right, next to me. Agent Cardinal, the wiry redhead who'd worked on the nursing-home case with us, sat next to Will. Such a small cavalry. How would we track Owen down in a hurry? Being a witch, he could be anywhere in the world.

Ma'am's fingers stilled, and she folded her hands in front of her. "Right. Lily, you're off Gus detail."

"What? No!" As much as I dreaded what Gus might talk about at times, he needed me, and so did both his bosses. What if that spell didn't stop till it got what it wanted? Surely there was time to help find Owen and protect Gus's two bosses?

"Yes." Something edgy strained from beneath her poker face. Her tone was dead. "I'm afraid Moira choked again last night at home. She's dead. Gus will be getting his promotion." Her jaw ticked as she jammed it shut. Imani's sharp intake of breath punctuated the shockwave vibrating through the room. Even Will's forehead wrinkles deepened.

My eyes flew open. *God no, no, no.* I shook my head over and over. I should have been there. We should have realised his magic could follow the victims anywhere. How did we not figure it out? Poor Moira. I didn't really know her, but she seemed nice enough, and she was innocent—just someone with a job who needed to be out of the way so Owen's prediction could come true.

The rage in my belly bubbled and spat, an acid storm of fury. "Does Gus know?" He was going to be devastated. He'd blame himself. Would he even take the promotion? What if it was too much, and he quit? So much for Owen's bloody predictions. My cheeks heated, and my magic called to me. It was telling me a lightning bolt would be a good idea. Smiting Owen would be fun. Everyone should get to be God for a day.

I jammed my teeth together. No. I wouldn't give in. *That's not who you are, Lily.* Plus I'd be the biggest moron ever, killing him before he could save Liv.

Imani drew her brows down as she stared at me. "Lily? Are you okay?"

I blinked some of the red haze from my eyes and met her scrutiny. "Gus is going to blame himself. Not to mention, that poor woman didn't deserve to die, and her family. Oh my God, how are they going to cope? This is…. It's just…." The back of my throat and nose prickled as tears threatened. I squeezed my hands into fists, channelled my thoughts to the sting of my nails biting into my palms.

What if Olivia were next?

Ma'am put her hands on her lap, took a deep breath, and addressed me. "We're not having that conversation, Lily. It's not your problem, and you're not to take it on board. Your job is to help these agents find Owen and bring him to us unharmed. Whatever his magic is doing, he needs to stop it. No one else can, at least not in time to save a lot of people heartache." I opened my mouth to speak, but she held up a warning palm. "We can't assume everyone will die, but they may lose jobs, or end up with injuries etcetera. But, yes, some will die to facilitate his predictions. Whether it's intentional or not is irrelevant. We need to get him here and make him disarm his spells."

Agent Cardinal leaned forward. "How are we doing this? Do we have any leads?"

"As a matter of fact, yes. He's appearing tonight in one of his biggest shows to date. He's at the London Coliseum."

Agent Cardinal whistled what I assumed was awe. "Impressive." I glowered at him. There was nothing impressive about Owen—he was a narcissistic fraud. He caught my look and jerked back. *That's right, buddy. I'm looking at you.* Owen wasn't getting even a millimetre of goodwill from me. Being famous didn't make you worthwhile. Why did people get caught up in that crap? If someone was horrible, I didn't care how talented they were; I'd rather support someone who was also a decent human.

Ma'am cleared her throat and raised her brow at me. I gave her a "what?" look. She ignored me and said, "I'd rather take him in well before he gets to the venue. As soon as possible, actually. Time is of the essence, considering all the lives at stake. I'm hoping this will be an easy arrest, since he has no idea we're even investigating him. But use caution. You'll need to put those cuffs on quickly, or he could disappear."

I couldn't help but sneer. "He's so arrogant, he'd probably still turn up for his show. But by then, how many more people could be dead or hurt?"

"Exactly. So, here's his home address. We've had people outside, but, of course, if he's travelled anywhere this morning, he won't be inside. We've only just put a catch spell on there because, obviously, we didn't know earlier what we know right now. We may have missed our chance, but we'll see."

"If he's not there, where else are we looking?" asked Will.

"He may even be at the Coliseum, preparing. He does have an assistant who works from an office in London. Here's the address. Agent Cardinal can cover the office— that's the least likely place he'll be. The assistant is a witch, but I doubt she has any idea of what Owen's up to. She'll hopefully be helpful. We'll need to bring her in for questioning anyway." The tingle of Ma'am's magic grazed my neck, and three pieces of paper appeared on the desk in front of Will; another piece of paper sat in front of Cardinal. "These are the search and arrest warrants. Because of the urgent nature, I've had our agents set up a landing point at Owen's address. Bring him in first. If he's not there, go to the theatre."

At least there wouldn't be any driving time. That would save hours, at least as far as going to London was concerned. "Where does he live?"

"Oxshott. It's about thirty miles west of here. It's an extensive property. We've set up the landing spot just outside the front gates, but as it's set back from the street, there should be no problem. If anyone sees it, we'll mindwipe. Not ideal, but we have to do what we have to do. Any questions?"

"Um, why exactly do I have to be there? It's not like I can arrest anyone. Won't I just be in the way?" I chewed a fingernail. Other than messing up, I didn't know how I'd react to seeing him. What if I lost it?

"You can tell if he's about to unleash a spell. If you feel his magic, I want you to yell *block*, and with some luck, Imani can cast a contain spell, but she'll have to be quick. It will stop him from releasing more magic or going anywhere. If we do this right, we'll get him in the cuffs without problems."

Imani nodded, her expression grave. Why so serious? It seemed straightforward enough. I guessed agents had to assume the worst was going to happen, and maybe she was just terrified we'd lose him and not save Liv. Which was fair enough. She wasn't the only one. And how long did Liv have left? I swallowed the bile that rose up my throat.

Stop thinking. I had to focus on my job now, which was to help bring Owen in.

"Before you leave, uniforms please, Lily and Imani."

"Okay," I said. Imani just nodded. I hesitated. I'd never changed using magic in front of anyone. What if something went wrong and I got stuck in my underwear? "Can I just duck to the bathroom?"

Ma'am drew her brows down. "Whatever for? You can get changed here. Stop being ridiculous. You're wasting time."

Fine. I sighed and took a deep breath, then requested a clothes swap. My jeans, jumper, and coat disappeared, and I was left standing in regulation black suit, tie, and white shirt. Thank God. I syphoned a tiny bit more magic and asked for my coat back—it was cold outside, and who knew how long we'd be out there.

Ma'am stood, and everyone else followed. "Go one at a time, Lily last." Golden numbers appeared in my head. I made my door and slapped them on. Will went first, and then Imani.

My body was on high alert as I stepped through into the freezing rain. Four agents awaited us under a canopy of skeletal trees. Gravel crunched as I turned to take it all in. The road was about twenty metres away. We stood between it and the grand brick-and-iron front gates, which gave access to a long drive flanked by trees and parkland. About fifty metres in sat one of the largest houses I'd ever seen.

Two stories of historical mansion, with ivy growing over the lower level, and a fountain in the middle of the circular driveway near the front doors. He didn't deserve to live in such gorgeous surroundings.

Business was certainly booming for our evil fortune teller. Hopefully it was all about to end.

Will chatted to a shorter, beefy agent who must have been in charge. "Any movement?"

"No. All quiet. The catch spell hasn't been triggered. We've magically disarmed the video surveillance. We did that yesterday as soon as we were on the job." He gave a nod to the camera trained in our direction sitting on the top of the gate. "So, how are we playing this?"

"Magic the gate open and drive in. Two of your guys can stay here, the other two go around the back. My guys will cover the front." An earpiece appeared in Will's ear, and he tapped it. "I'll give you the signal to go in when we're ready. And we take him alive and in as good a state as possible. This is critical." Will didn't divert his gaze from the agent until he'd given a firm nod.

"Understood." He turned to his men, gave them orders, then motioned towards the street. "Van's over here."

"I've got the gate," Imani said, gesturing towards it. It clicked, then slowly opened.

We followed the agent to the white van on the street. He hopped into the passenger side. His partner, a tall bald guy, slipped into the driver's seat. Will, Imani, and I jumped into the back of the van. I slid the door closed. We lurched forward at speed, gravel spray chinking against the chassis. I tripped and fell backwards, crashing into Imani. She caught me with a grunt.

"Oops. Sorry." I put a hand on the side of the van to steady myself.

"It's okay. Just be ready when we get out." Her firm grip on my arms was harder than it needed to be, and her expression was grim. I'd never seen her so stressed about an assignment—not that I'd seen her on a lot of jobs, but still. She wasn't her usual cool-and-collected self. She didn't release me until we'd come to a skidding halt in the turning circle in front of the entry.

I connected with the river of power as I jumped out—I was not going to muck this up.

Black suits ran to their positions. The house was so large that the agents sprinting around the back had a long way to run. Will and Imani took up places on either side of the front door, guns drawn. Will motioned me to get behind him. I wasn't going to argue.

"We're in position." Will must've been talking to the other agent, but he didn't get an answer straight away. My heart did its best to try and beat its way out. The rush of my blood swooshing past my eardrums blocked out almost all other sound.

We waited.

Imani focussed solely on Will, waiting for his signal. Something flashed in his eyes, and he gave her the nod. Her magic swept over my scalp, and the door slammed open. They rushed in, guns held out in front. Will yelled, "This is the PIB. Owen Thomas Small-Cox, show yourself!" His voice echoed in the large, stone-tiled vestibule. A nervous snort exploded from my nose. Mr Self-Important had the most ridiculous name. No wonder he didn't use it. Small-Cox. Seemed fitting.

Silence. I strained all my senses, waiting for any hint of Owen's power. But if it came now, how would Imani be able to stop him since she couldn't see him? She wouldn't know where to direct her spell.

Will spoke into his wrist piece. It was like being in a movie with American government operatives. How did my life get this surreal? I totally needed a holiday. "We'll clear the south wing; you clear the north. Then we'll head upstairs." As he slipped to the left through a doorway, he said over his shoulder, "Stay with me. And put up your return-to-sender."

Ah, crap. Rookie mistake. I'd forgotten again. I threw it up and followed, Imani behind me. Will called out again, "PIB, show yourself, Owen Thomas Small-Cox!"

Will and Imani's footsteps were almost silent as we hurried over the swanky parquet floors, through high-ceilinged rooms full of expensive paintings, furniture, and knickknacks. This guy was out to impress, if the fresco-ceilinged ballroom was anything to go by.

Eventually, we were back in the entryway, no sign of Mr Small-Cox anywhere. Will pointed, and we ventured up the sweeping staircase. He called out again, but there was no answer. We rushed through one bedroom, then another, and another. Nothing. When we'd covered it all, Will spoke into his wrist. "All clear. Copy." The other agent must have responded because then he said, "You stay here. If he happens to come back, cuff him and let me know straight away. Remember: take him alive. We're going to the theatre."

At least once he was back here, he couldn't travel out again—he'd be trapped, but still, a cornered rat might try anything, so he was still dangerous. And what if someone accidentally killed him before we could get him to remove his spells?

Liv would die.

I swallowed against the nausea rolling up my throat.

Will gave Imani a nod, then looked at me. "Okay, let's go. We'll have to travel from the front gates so we don't get caught in the catch spell." He jogged away from us, and we followed. At the gates, Will made the doorway. "You come with me, Lily." He grabbed my hand, and we stepped through into a clean bathroom stall. He flicked the lock up, and we hurried out, leaving room for Imani to come through. At the main bathroom door into the theatre, Will hesitated while she caught up.

Will pulled a piece of paper out of his pocket and unfolded it before pointing to the different areas. "Here's a map of the place. Performer changing rooms are here. His show is happening in here. I would think he'd be in one of those two places. We'll have to stay together because we need Lily to tell us if he's casting a spell."

I didn't want to hold things up, but I had to know. "Why didn't Ma'am put a catch spell on this place too?"

Will spoke quickly, likely wanting to get on with it. "It

would take too long. This place is huge. It would've been a mammoth effort to set up the one at his home, so we used resources there. This one would take three or four witches an hour to set up. We just didn't have time."

"Okay. Sorry. Just wanted to know." If I didn't ask questions, how would I ever learn? As much as Angelica was meant to be my mentor, she didn't often stop to explain things unless I asked. If I'd left it up to her, I'd know pretty much almost nothing.

"Protocol for bystanders?" Imani asked.

"Hang on." Will pulled out his phone and dialled. "Ma'am. Yes…. No…. We're at the Coliseum. We're not sure, but we may need mindwipes. I haven't got a number, no." He stared past me as she spoke. After a minute, he said, "Okay. Will do. Bye." He addressed Imani. "She's sending a standby team of four. They'll deploy in ten minutes so we can keep the magic pings to a minimum." Travelling didn't make too much *noise* as far as spells went, but if there were a few witches coming through, maybe it was louder. How loud had we been? Did he know something was going on? Nah, surely he wouldn't have any idea. He'd just be getting ready for his show, oblivious. I growled. Oblivious to my best friend dying in her hospital room. Oblivious to the woman who had died last night. My veins turned to ice—how she must have felt, trying to breathe and not able to get it in, knowing she was choking *again*. The whole thing was horrific.

Will pinned me with an intense battleship-grey stare.

"No-notice spell on now. Stay behind Imani. And you have only *one* job—tell Imani if he casts a spell. Okay?"

I nodded firmly while adding my no-notice spell to my return-to-sender, hoping he could see in my eyes that I meant it—I was going to behave, only do what they'd asked, because, yes, I had a history of going rogue. I was not going to stuff this up. My friend's life was at risk. If I messed up, it would be my fault she died. My heart rate kicked up a notch, and I had to take a couple of slow breaths. The best thing I could do right now was block out what was at stake; otherwise I'd be useless.

Will opened the door and stuck his head through, checking before entering the hallway. Imani followed, and I went after her. We jogged down the hallway, the air imbued with the lingering perfume of a thousand dressed-up theatregoers and time-worn architecture.

Unfortunately, there were people wandering about—a couple of workers, and a handful of people roaming through, admiring the opulence of the high patterned ceilings and old-world ambiance. Not many, but enough that maybe they'd notice something going down if it were loud enough. Will seemed to ignore them all though as he kept his focus ahead.

He turned right, and we entered a low-lit corridor. Every now and then, I jerked my head around to look over my shoulder. No one followed. I tried to keep my awareness on everything around me, waiting for that telltale sign of magic. Although if he cast a spell now, it wouldn't be anything to do with us. I guessed I had to worry about it when he knew we were here. But if I felt his magic, it would mean he was definitely here. Will hadn't heard from Agent Cardinal, so Owen mustn't have been at the office. But what if his assistant alerted him? Crap. Surely Cardinal wouldn't let that happen. Gah, I had to trust that the professionals knew what they were doing. Second-guessing them would get me nothing but an ulcer.

Please be here. Please be here.

We reached the end of the hallway and a door that said Changing Rooms. Will put his ear to the door and listened. Then he turned the handle and shoved the door open. We entered a bland white-painted room with three doors off it. Will and Imani approached each door in turn, possibly deciding which one to go into.

I stood back, practically holding my breath and just being aware. A faint breath of magic tickled the back of my neck. I shuddered. It wasn't his magic. I whispered, "There's another witch here. They just did something."

They looked at me. Will's wrinkles were as fierce as ever. He whispered, "I felt it. Do you recognise it?"

"No." There it was again, brushing down my spine this time.

Will must have noticed my shiver. "Can you tell where it's coming from?"

I looked at each door, although that would never give me the answer. It didn't feel as if that's where it had emanated from. I looked at the ceiling. "I think it's above us… somewhere. Maybe over there a bit. I pointed to the wall. "The actual theatre area maybe?"

Will nodded. "Okay. Well, we still have to clear these rooms. You said it wasn't him, right?"

"Yes, as in, no; it wasn't him." So confusing. Lucky I wasn't running this show.

"Right." He turned to Imani. "We'll take one each. Whoever gets out here first can take the last one."

She gave him a nod and raised her gun. As one door slammed open, then the other, and they rushed in, I backed up against the wall so I could see all the doors and the corridor we'd just walked through and not worry about someone sneaking up behind me. Within thirty seconds, they were back out. They gave each other a nod, as if to say, all clear. Then Will forced open the last door and entered. Imani stood guard outside it.

The magic tingled again, and it was definitely coming from above us.

A woman screamed, "Get out!" Will backed out of the door, a rotund older lady pushing him. I wasn't sure what was bigger: her yellow beehive hairdo or her ample stomach. "These are private quarters. I don't know what show you're from, but this area is out of bounds. Be out with your fool self." She gave him a final shove and slammed the door. He turned to look at me, a harried expression on his face. Imani snorted, and I bit back a smile.

He ran a hand through his hair and straightened his tie. When he'd composed himself, he turned to Imani. "All clear."

Her lip quirked up on one side. "Almost, apparently."

I wished we could joke about the encounter, but Liv was

dying right now, and, well… that was it, really. "I felt the magic again. Upstairs."

"Right. The only place left is the theatre. If he's not there…." Imani straightened her shoulders against the implied despair in what she'd said. *If he's not there, where the hell was he, and would we find him in time? I blew out a sigh and reset. Don't think. Just do.*

I started down the hallway, back the way we'd come. "We can't find him standing around. Come on."

Will pushed past me to lead, and Imani stayed behind me. I kept my feelers out for magic. Back in the main corridor, a few more people filed past, chatting, laughing. Oblivious. Will touched his earpiece, stopped abruptly, and turned. The opposite way to where we were going must be the front entrance because four agents were striding down the hallway. Must be the mindwipe team. Would that be the official name? It would be kinda cool on a card: Byron Smith, Manager, Mindwipe Division.

Will gave them a nod, then pivoted. We resumed our trek towards the theatre. Then the doors were there, looming. I swallowed. This had to go well. He had to be there. *Please be there.*

My heart raced as Will put his palm on the door and pushed.

I sucked in a breath. *Wow.* We weren't here on a sight-seeing tour, but as I searched for Owen, the majesty of the space was impossible to ignore. Three stories of balconies rose towards the domed ceiling. Maroon and red velvet, bronze and gold trimmings, from the rows upon rows of plush seats to the incredibly detailed walls and ceiling to the orchestra pit and stage, opulent didn't begin to describe it. And standing in the middle of the stage talking to two men was something that didn't belong amongst such grandeur.

Mr Small-Cox.

I wasn't going to call him by what he wanted since being self-important was what he was all about. He'd killed to maintain the status quo, even if it was indirectly. The simmering heat of my anger intensified. The bubbling began in my stomach, sending fire through my veins. He was not getting away. The only positive of this situation was that he was here. Our search had ended, thank God.

He spied us and stopped speaking. The other men with him were dressed head to toe in black. I recognised them as his handlers, the ones from Liv's party. Small-Cox put his hands on his hips and raised his voice. "This theatre is off limits. You'll have to leave, or I'll call security."

Will headed towards the stage and raised his gun. "I'm afraid we won't be leaving for a moment." My shoulders tensed. How was Owen going to react to the threat? His two goons hurried towards the front of the stage where a black ramp covered the distance from the stage across the orchestra pit. Two different magics feathered my nape. I shuddered. Gross. It was like being touched by someone I didn't know. Ew. Owen's magic wasn't in the mix… yet. But why didn't Imani just try and freeze him anyway? Strike before there was a real need to. Wasn't she allowed? Kind of like a police officer could only shoot under certain circumstances? And UK police didn't even carry guns… but the PIB did, and they currently had them trained on the stage.

Imani glanced at me, a questioning look on her face. I shook my head. "There are two witches using magic, but not him."

"Okay, thanks." She and Will walked carefully towards the side of the stage with the ramp. I stayed behind them, my gaze never leaving Owen.

He kept his hands on his hips, elbows out like a rooster trying to assert dominance as he observed us down the length of his nose. "What are you still doing here?"

Will was closer to the stage. Owen's men had traversed the ramp. They jumped down to the bottom level of the theatre and headed towards Will and Imani with arrogant strides. One of them said, "You can't be in here. You need to leave. Now."

Will lifted his gun, pointed it at them. "Stop right there." His gaze flicked to Owen, then back to his two guys who'd probably worked out by now that we were witches—took them long enough. They were likely too busy being arrogant to worry about it before. No one had thrown a spell, which would be nuts since we all had our return-to-senders up. I crossed my fingers it would stay that way.

Imani edged around the side of the group so she and Will had the two men well and truly covered. She gave a chin tip. "We're from the PIB. Put your hands on your heads and turn around."

The slightly taller goon stopped, but he didn't make any move to put his hands on his head. "You can't just come in here and do that. Where's your warrant? How do I even know you're actually from the PIB?"

Will's magic tickled my scalp, and the arrest warrant floated in the air, unfolded, and hovered close enough for the guy to read it. Will hadn't stated anything about Owen being under arrest yet—it must be because he didn't want him to try and run, but he had to say it at some point. Before the guy could get a great look at the paper, it disappeared. Well played, Will.

The other guy looked back at his boss, who'd lowered his arms. Was he getting ready to run? He must have been wondering what was happening. Did he even know what his magic had been doing to people? And if he did, did he even care?

Imani's voice rang out loudly across the theatre. "Put your hands on your heads and turn around."

"Not until you tell us who's under arrest." The first guy was not going down without at least an argument. Damn that guy.

My phone vibrated in my pocket. Without taking my eyes off Owen, I pulled it out. Oh, crap. I was going to have to take my eyes off Owen. What if the message was important? I lifted the phone so I still had him in the background. It was from Beren. As I read it, dread iced my skin.

We're losing her, Lily. I'm doing my best, but I can't hold her here much longer. The spell's gone into overdrive. I'm going to burn out trying to save her. B.

It was as if I were falling into a chasm. The horror of having a minute to know you were about to die and not being able to do anything about it was excruciating, but in this case, my friend was the one facing oblivion. My stomach dropped, and my head spun. This had to happen right now.

"She's dying, Will. She's almost gone."

My words triggered something in Owen. He stared at me, but rather than shock or fear, it was anger, like I'd gone and messed up his birthday party by forgetting the cake or opening his present for him. His magic pinged my spine. "Imani. He's using it!"

Power assaulted me, peppering my scalp as everyone unleashed. So much for return-to-senders being able to stop everything.

Imani threw her hands towards Owen. His magic stopped flowing, and he stood stiffly, unmoving. One of Owen's thugs leapt for Will, while the other fired a spell at him. Will's gun went off as he flew backwards. One of the bad guys also careened backwards—whatever he'd hit Will with must have returned to him. The other guy had stopped coming after Will and stared at Imani. His lips moved as he cast another spell. But why? She had her— Oh, crap. She didn't. I looked at her aura, and she had no defensive spells set. The only spell she had was the one she was using on Owen. Were they mutually exclusive? Is that why she'd held off? Is that why she'd been overly stressed?

A force slammed into Imani, lifting her off her feet and flinging her across the room. She landed on her back on the top of a red velvet seat with a heavy grunt and crack. Owen, free of her spell, turned and ran. Will and Imani were down, but I couldn't let him get away.

And there it was. I almost choked at the feel of his magic. I imagined my power was a net, and I threw it at him. "Stop Owen from leaving the building." I wanted to say not to travel or not to run, but that would have taken too long. I should've just frozen him, but after what happened to Imani, I figured I wouldn't be able to keep my return-to-sender up.

I sprinted towards the ramp. Another tingle of power jagged along my scalp—the witch who'd spelled Imani was drawing magic again, but Will was struggling to stand, his gun aiming for him. I couldn't wait to see or help—if they couldn't deal with this, what good would I be? Will's gaze met mine, and he gave me a nod. As much as I hated leaving them—and God knew if Imani was even alive—Liv and a whole lot of others needed me to catch Owen. It was up to me to bring him down, and Will agreed.

Challenge accepted.

As I bolted across the ramp and onto the stage, Owen disappeared through the curtain. A gunshot rang out behind me, but I ignored it and kept going. The force of Owen's magic trying to break free was like little cockroach claws scratching against my magic. Yuck.

My footfalls echoed as I jumped over the cables that snaked across the stage. I dodged a microphone stand and two chairs, then shoved the heavy curtain aside as I followed Owen's thudding footsteps. He could run, but he couldn't hide. My net linked us, and I could feel where he was.

It was darker back here, and it took a moment for my eyes to adjust. There were a few large crates, a closed roller door, and not much else. I hurried through a doorway into another corridor. I followed the invisible string linking me to Owen.

My breaths were loud as I sucked in air. Dizziness engulfed me. I stopped and slapped my palm on the wall to keep from falling. What the hell? Was I using too much magic by holding the net around him? Whatever it was, I'd just have to deal. As soon as I caught him, everything would be fine. I could sleep for a week if I wanted, but now wasn't the time to succumb to the yawn that widened my jaw. I took a deep breath, steadied myself, and set off.

A short way along the hall was a door that called to me —or, rather, the net around the person behind it did. I reached for the doorknob, but then two pulses of magic pinged my spine—Will and one of the bad guys. My heart skipped in fear. What was going on back there? A loud crack sounded. Another gunshot. Crap. No more time to waste.

I turned the handle and opened the door.

It was even darker in here than the hallway. There were two windows on a wall to my left, both covered by thick blinds. The little light seeping in made shadowed shapes of the furniture and boxes. It looked to be a large, old office-cum-storage room.

Goosebumps peppered my arms. He was in here. So close. Against every survival instinct, I stepped all the way in and shut the door—I didn't want him running again. Time was as much my enemy as Owen.

Should I just call out and tell him to show himself? If he could feel me through the net like I could feel him, he'd know I knew he was here. But if he didn't realise I could sense him, it would give me an advantage. But then, searching for him would waste time.

A throb started in my temple, and it was as if someone were pushing me away. It was the slightest sensation. Was that Owen feeling for a way out of my net? Another dizzy spell hit, and I swayed. It took everything I had not to drop to the floor.

Decision made.

I forced as much strength as I could into my voice—show no weakness, pretend I'm the most powerful witch who ever lived. *Yeah, ha ha.* Hopefully, he wouldn't see through my ruse. "Owen, show yourself. I'm not leaving here without you." Silence met my demand, my words falling dead around me. I moved further into the room and stopped to listen. "Your stupid magic is killing my friend. If she dies, you'll be going to jail forever." I decided not to mention the fact that he would anyway since his magic had killed a ton of other people. A man with nothing to lose would be even more dangerous. "So just stop wasting my time and show yourself. As I said: I'm not leaving here without you."

I took a few more steps and stopped. It was near impossible to tell if he lingered behind the boxes to my right, or under the desk in front of me. Or was he in that cupboard that sat against the far wall? I supposed I'd have to methodically check one after the other. But what was I going to do when I caught him? *Jesus, Lily.* I could've slapped myself for being so stupid. Who comes this far without a plan? Me, apparently…. To be fair to myself, I'd thought Will and Imani would be taking him in.

Right. Think. I had a spell that stopped Owen from leaving the premises, which meant I'd have to quickly drop that so I could take him through my doorway, and I'd have to do that by dragging him. If he struggled against me and accidentally touched my doorway, he'd potentially die or lose a limb, and then he wouldn't be in any state to reverse the spell killing Liv. And if I dropped the spell without having control of him, he could just leave via his own doorway. Argh! Why did this have to be so difficult? Maybe I could just make an extra-big doorway around us? That might take too much power, but maybe it wouldn't. I'd just have to try because I had nothing else. I ignored the universe when it prodded me with its bony finger of despair.

My head jerked to the left. Had that been a rustle of fabric or a breath? As much as I wanted to head to the boxes to see, I was going to check under the desk first. If I headed to the boxes, I'd leave a clear pathway to the door from the desk. Not a wise move.

I crept towards the table, ignoring the power buffeting my senses. Whatever was going on out there was some kind of epic battle. Not good. I stepped around the table, my heart thudding loudly. Damn. I leaned over carefully, quietly. Part of the underneath of the table was in my line of sight, but it was too dark under there to see anything. Crap. I supposed I could risk reaching out and feeling for him because there wasn't a gap big enough for him to squeeze through—the front of the table facing the door had a panel that went almost to the floor.

Holding my breath and straining both eyes and ears, I reached under the table. Cold air feathered my fingers. I silently, slowly breathed out in relief. I bent in further just to make sure, but, nope, he wasn't under there. That left the boxes.

I straightened. A wave of tiredness crashed over me, and I momentarily shut my eyes. *Come on, Lily. You're almost there.* I opened my eyes and crept back around to the front of the desk. There was that prod against my power. It was as if someone was pushing against my brain or thoughts. Hard to describe, but I just knew it was Owen testing the net. As he did, vibrations of his magic skittered over my scalp. I shuddered. He may not be able to escape, but he could still cast a spell. My return-to-sender was up, but it was an effort to keep it there. Sweat tickled my forehead. What if he just punched me or used his magic to throw the table into me and knocked me out? Unconscious, all my spells would disappear. But was he strong enough? The spells he had out in the world killing and maiming must have been getting sustenance from somewhere. Either he was incredibly powerful, or he was close to burning himself out to keep it all going. Or had he managed to develop some kind of method where he tied off the source to the spells so they only tried two or three times to obtain the objective of making the person's dreams come true? Kind of like three wishes from a genie. Even so, he'd be using a mass of power.

I would only know the answer if he told me. Time to get this guy.

As I noiselessly approached the pile of boxes, I delved into the river of power. *Oh.* There was a wide, fast-flowing rush of magic coming into me. Normally, it was much thinner, except when I was trying to kill Jeremy's mother. I'd put everything I had into that and almost died as a consequence. I must have gotten stronger since then. Thank the universe for small favours. There was no way I would've been able to manage all these spells simultaneously if I hadn't. But would one more spell tip me over the edge?

I was about to find out.

I reached the boxes and slid my phone out of my pocket. I'd need to see clearly to do this right. I flicked my phone to silent, unlocked it, and, as I stepped around the boxes, turned the torch function on.

Yes! Owen was crouched against the wall, making him look small, pathetic. I shone my light into his eyes. "Coward. Narcissist pig." Oh, okay, I hadn't expected to say that, but my anger came rushing to the surface, way hotter than my magic. "Stand up. You're coming with me to the PIB. You have to take back your spells."

He blinked up at me and shielded his eyes with his hand. He slowly stood, and I stepped back, his eyes gleaming with malice. He spat at me. My eyes widened. "Oh my God, you're gross. What the hell is wrong with you?"

He sneered. "You're messing with the wrong witch. I've stepped over far better than you on my way to the top, and no snivelling Aussie convict is going to tell me what to do.

I'm a god among men. I grant people their wildest desires, and some that aren't so wild. They worship me. Do you know how hard I've worked to get here?" I opened my mouth to respond, but he kept talking. "I've sacrificed for this my entire life. I'm finally where I deserve to be, and I haven't finished yet. No one, least of all you, is taking my magnificent future away from me."

Power pulsed from him. Sharpness, like the blade of a knife, sliced into my stomach. I doubled over and grunted. He'd tried to break through my net spell, and because he hadn't thrown a spell at me, my return-to-sender was no protection. Jeez was his magic strong. He went to push past me. No way, mate. This Aussie convict wasn't a quitter.

I stuck my foot out. He caught it and went down. *Take that, fraudster.* My eyes were still watering from the magic sucker punch, but I didn't care. I hobbled to where he was trying to stand, and he pushed me. I tripped backwards but managed to keep my feet. He stood and headed for the door. *Not so fast.*

I sprinted, overtaking him, then turned at the last second and slammed my back against the door. "You're not going anywhere but to help my friend."

He faced me, a look of disgust on his face. His calculating gaze figured I was just one small blip between him and the corridor to freedom. "Are you going to move, or am I going to have to lay hands on you? Don't make me. It won't be pretty."

I tilted my chin up. "Nothing about this is pretty, trust me. And you're the least attractive thing about it. You're the equivalent of someone who's bought their way into an art prize, or a sports person who's a drug cheat. You're just a dishonest loser. If it wasn't for your magic, none of that stuff would come true, would it? You're a fraud." I angled my phone so the light shone in his eyes. Take that, craphead. He was still a little bit too far in front of me for what I was going to do. I had to get right next to him and quickly build the doorway. But he had other ideas.

He lunged for me and slapped his hands on my shoulders while simultaneously assaulting the net. He threw me to the side, and shooting pain gored my middle as I landed on the floor. He reached for the door handle, then opened the door.

Tears from the pain coursed down my face, but I wasn't giving up. The net held, thank God. He took one step through the door. I gave it everything I had and lunged to grab his ankle. I wrapped my hands tightly around it and squeezed. I was going to be a leech to the death.

He tried to shake me off. I mumbled my doorway spell, hoping I'd allowed enough room for his head—since I was on the ground, it was hard to tell how tall it should be—stuck the coordinates to the PIB on it, then dropped the net spell. The river of power turned into rapids as it gushed into me.

Everything spun into black.

***

. . .

THERE WAS A MAD RUSHING IN MY EARS AND PRESSURE ON MY throat. An alarm blared, but it sounded far away, maybe outside. I was tired, so tired. I forced my eyes open. Red-faced, Owen kneeled next to me, his enraged eyes boring into mine while he strangled me.

I hooked my fingers under his hands, but there was no way they'd budge. Panic buzzed through the fog in my head. Air. I needed air.

"I'm not letting you ruin everything, convict scum. I have a sold-out show tonight, and I'm going on."

What was it with the constant convict insults? I gasped out, "You have no imagination." He contorted his face as he squeezed harder. If I could've told him what a loser he was, I would have, but even though my lips moved, my voice was throttled by his grip. Looks like they would be my last words. Ever.

A slamming sound, far away. God, I needed a breath. I dug my nails into his skin. Magic, where was my magic? The edges of my vision darkened—such a cliché, but it was a thing. Who knew?

Owen's face disappeared… so did the pressure on my neck. "Lily, Lily!" I was jostled. Air gushed into my mouth, throat, then lungs. The encroaching blackness brightened. I sat up, coughing. After every cough, I sucked in sweet, sweet air, more delicious than a double-chocolate muffin. I'd never thought I'd see the day where I'd say anything was more delicious than that, but there you go—there really was a first time for everything. James crouched next to me, concern in his eyes, his hand on my back. "What year is it?"

I croaked out a "huh?" I was so happy to see him, but why was he asking me this? "Owen. Where's Owen?" My head jerked around. We were in the PIB reception room, and Owen wasn't there. A zing of adrenaline shot through my stomach. "Oh my God, James. We have to find Owen. He was just here." My voice was a lot quieter than I'd intended. Being choked really put a dampener on things. I tried to stand, but James put his hand on my shoulder and forced me to stay. "Stop, James! Liv's dying. We have to find Owen." I slapped his hand out of the way and tried to get up again, but my legs were too jelly, and I sat back down with a thud.

"We're on it. Angelica has him in custody—arrested just then in fact, mid strangling you. They're taking him to the hospital to see Liv now."

Right, so I'd gotten as far as the PIB, but I must've used too much magic and blacked out, which meant we'd only just arrived. I sighed out my relief. I'd gotten him here in time. I looked up to the ceiling. *Thank you, Universe, but you better make sure he saves Liv.* I looked at my brother. "What if he refuses to save her?"

"I don't think that's an option." His mouth quirked up in a grim smile.

"What do you mean?"

"You don't wanna know."

Did that mean they would stoop to threats and torture? Somehow that didn't bother me in the least. My eyes widened. "Oh my God! Will and Imani! They were battling it out with Owen's henchmen. We have to help them. There were other agents there, but I have no idea what they were up to. They were there for the mindwiping later, but Imani was down, and Will was struggling."

"It's okay. We're onto that. About two minutes before you got here, one of them called in the magic use and gunshots." James's phone rang. He pulled it out of his pocket and stood. He made a few "I'm listening" noises. "Okay, thanks. Bye." He turned to me. "Will and Imani are in with our healers. Let's go see how they're doing." James bent, grabbed my hand, and helped me up.

I took a second to steady my legs. Drained didn't even begin to describe how I felt. "Did they catch Owen's thugs?"

"Will killed one with his gun, the other is in custody. So, tell me what happened." As we ambled slowly to the medical rooms in the PIB—I couldn't walk much faster than a shuffle—I gave James a rundown of what had happened. The whole time I talked, though, all I could do was worry. Were Imani and Will really going to be okay? Would Owen stop that spell from killing Liv, or would Ma'am's plan—whatever it was—fail? It wasn't as if she were a god. Maybe she threatened his life, but he was an arrogant bastard. Maybe he'd choose to die over admitting he'd cheated to make his predictions come true.

We arrived at the infirmary. James pushed open the door and led the way in. Somehow I knew Will was okay. Our connection on the magical plane—the connection that meant we could talk mind to mind—meant I could feel if he was alive. I'd discovered that in the warehouse incident when the snake group kidnapped Will. If it wasn't for that,

I'd be a basket case about now. It was also a good sign that both he and Imani had made it this far. The witch healers were incredible and could work miracles. If they were here, it was likely they'd be fine.

We walked through a sterile white room with a couple of waiting-room-type chairs, an empty hospital bed on wheels, and filing cabinets. The next room was where it was at, *it* being all the good stuff. Will and Imani both lay on hospital beds that sat against the far wall. They were awake and smiling. I ran to Will and threw my arms around him; professionalism could go to hell right now. He was warm, ruffled, but alive. I breathed him in and snuggled into his chest. My voice came out muffled. "I'm so glad you're okay. What did those guys do to you?"

He stroked my head. "Nothing I couldn't handle. But what about you? You ran off after our friend. The only reason I didn't go after you is, I could feel you were okay."

I released my grip on his warmness and straightened, looking across his bed to Imani, who was watching us with half-closed eyes. "You okay?"

She nodded and gave a sleepy smile. "Yeah, but, boy, do I have a sore back."

The witch in a white lab coat with a stethoscope dangling around his neck said, "She's one very lucky witch. She was almost a paraplegic. We could have cured it, of course, but even with magic, it's never a perfect job, and she would have had months of rehab. Anyway, I'll leave you to your reunion." He left the room, which was good because even though he was an agent, maybe some of what we had to say was confidential.

I scrunched my face and cringed. "The way you landed on that chairback, I'm not surprised. It was painful to watch." I shook my head—she'd come close to losing her life, but she hadn't, and now we only had one person to worry about.

Will grabbed my hand. "So, what happened?"

"Oh, um, I managed to find Owen hiding in an office. I brought him back here, but I'd used so much magic that I passed out. I came to while he was strangling me."

Imani gasped. "Oh my goodness, love. Are you okay?"

I shrugged and rubbed my still-sore neck. "I'm standing here, so I guess so." I smiled. "Ironic though—waking up while being strangled."

James scowled. "It's not funny, Lily. If we hadn't gotten to you when we did…."

"But you did, and I'm fine. Anyway, Ma'am's taken him to Liv's, to cure her."

"What if he refuses?" Imani asked.

"That's what I said." My gut twisted. What if he wasn't cooperating? She might already be dead. God, no. I looked at James. "Can we go see what's happening?"

He shook his head. "Just wait. Trust me."

I sat in a chair next to Will's bed. He and Imani were still exhausted after being healed, so we decided to wait it out right there. No one said a word for fifteen minutes. Then James's phone rang, and I started. We all stared at him as he answered. "Hello. Yes?" He nodded and bit his lip. "Mmhmm. Okay… yes, right. Bye." Gah, his poker face gave nothing away.

I leaned forward. "So? Spill." He stared at me a beat too long. The silence turned into a solid mass that sucked all the oxygen out of the room. My nose tingled with the pressure of impending tears. This couldn't be happening. He couldn't be telling me she didn't make it.

The outer door to the infirmary opened. Everyone stared at the door. A trolley nosed in, pushed by a droopy-shouldered, dark-under-eye-bagged Beren. On the bed, head propped up by pillows, was a wan but smiling Liv. My eyes widened. I jumped up. "Oh my God! You're okay!"

I ran to the trolley and practically threw myself onto the bed and gave her a hug. "You have no idea how worried we all were." I leaned back to look at her. Her face was even more gaunt than this morning, and her curls were limp and half the volume of normal. But she was alive. Alive! "What about your parents? How did you escape the hospital without them having a heart attack?"

Beren looked at me. "We had to mindwipe a lot of people and implant false memories. Ma'am is still there with the team. They'll be there for another hour or so. We've given Liv's parents the memory of me taking her to the hospital to see what was wrong. They'll be expecting me to drive her back in an hour. But she's cured."

"How did you get Small-Cox to do that?"

Liv scrunched her forehead. "Who's Small-Cox?"

"That was idiot fortune teller's real name." I was so angry, I wasn't going to be nice about him, not even to Liv."

She made a silent O with her lips. Although, after what he'd done to her, she likely wouldn't be a member of his fan club any longer.

"Anyway," Beren said, "he didn't agree. He wouldn't admit to anything, even though we had proof it was his magic. He was indignant and demanded we take him back to perform his show, even knowing Ma'am had caught him strangling Lily. He's a right nutter." He took a deep breath. "This doesn't leave this room. Understood?" We all nodded as he made a bubble of silence. "Ma'am coerced him. She got into his head and forced him to do it. She read his mind, then compelled him to comply. She's currently forcing him to undo dozens of spells. Once they've finished, he's going away for life."

Liv frowned, her eyes sad. "It's not all his fault. I gave him the idea. He was reading people's minds, seeing what their deepest wishes and desires were, then making them happen, no matter the cost. I wished I were skinny, that I could eat whatever I wanted and not put on weight. His spell gave me a metabolism that was so fast, it was killing me."

"Hey, it's not your fault!" I gave her a stern stare. "Stupid Kate bullied you for years. No wonder you worried about it, but you know what? You're gorgeous, and you weren't even chubby. And even if you were chubby, or fat, we would all still love you. You aren't your weight. You're a gorgeous girl outside because you are inside. And I never want you to change. I just want you to love you for you, like the rest of us do." I took her hand and smiled. "Think you can do that?"

She smiled. "I think I can. I'm definitely not dying to be slim." She chuckled. "Yeah, that was a bad joke, but now I see how crazy it was to put so much energy into worrying about it. I'm just glad it's all over. Oh, and Ma'am saw that Owen was responsible for Kate's death—his magic put more oomph into the push than I ever would have. They're going to have a word with our liaison at the Kent police, and they're charging him with her manslaughter." She sunk back into her pillows and sighed. "I'm so tired. I need a nap."

Beren gazed lovingly down at her. "Healing will do that to you, not to mention we need to get you a few good feeds. You're skin and bone."

"Lily." Will looked at me. "What do you say we go home? I'm exhausted, and you look like you could use a night on the couch too. We could order Indian." He grinned.

I'd only just had it at Liv's, but who cared? You could never get too much of a good thing, despite some people arguing to the contrary. "That sounds like heaven." I gave Liv another hug, then went and embraced Imani. Everyone was going to be fine, but we'd come so close to that not being the case. I looked around at Liv. "Oh, does that mean you're moving back in?"

She smiled. "Yep. I'll see you tomorrow, around lunchtime. Maybe you and Imani can pick up some yummy stuff from Costa, and we'll have a celebratory lunch at home and binge-watch *Stranger Things*. I doubt I'll be up to going out." I dared say she was right. I was surprised she had enough energy for this conversation. She was so thin, it was scary.

"Sounds like a plan." I grinned.

"I'm in," said Imani.

I turned to James. "What about the lady with the Christmas tree, and the dance kids? Oh, and that poor man who shot himself?"

"We're still working on it all, but the guy who shot himself, his daughter had gone to Owen. She needed money to pay back some debts. She inherited when her father died, so we're charging him with murder for that one. And, I imagine, the others will be linked to him too—maybe a parent wanted their kid to win the competition? And maybe the woman who died had relatives who would benefit? It will all be cleared up soon, but Beren, Will, and I have a gazillion interviews to carry out in the coming weeks."

Will groaned. "Oh, the joy." He looked at me. "Since I have so much work coming up, and I'm so very exhausted right now, can we go home?"

"Um, yes, in a sec. I have one more question." I turned back to my brother. "How's Mill? What are we going to do about the snake group?" That catch spell still had me spooked.

James scowled. "Yes, well, we're being extra cautious, but now this drama is over, we're going to have to have another meeting." He ran his gaze over everyone. "None of us are safe. I want you all to check for catch spells before you leave the house from now on. I hate to say it, Lily, but you're going to have to go back to Mum's diary, retrace her steps, and photograph everything you can. Make sure you take Will or Imani with you whenever you go out."

I rolled my eyes. "Yes, of course. As if I'm not doing that already. Sheesh." As awesome as it was to have everyone okay, my chest constricted with sadness. Seeing photos of my parents was both a curse and a blessing. Every time I saw them was emotionally draining, and now I was going to have to do it on a larger scale than before. I supposed the quicker I did it, the sooner we could find the Regula Pythonissam lair and discover what happened to my parents. Only then could James and I truly move on.

Will poked my side a few times. I looked at him. "Right. I guess I'd better get Agent Crankypants home before I get into trouble." I smirked. He hadn't been cranky much the last couple of weeks, but I enjoyed stirring him. He gave me a steely stare, but I noticed the twitch at one corner of his lips. "Are you right to make your own doorway?" I had to ask because I wasn't sure if I had enough energy left to make one large enough for both of us.

He swung his legs off the bed and stood. "I've got enough in the tank for way more than that." He waggled his eyebrows.

"Ew, man, don't go there in front of me. That's my sister."

Imani and I both snorted at the same time. "Jinx!" I said.

"What are you, twelve?" James looked at me.

"You're the one who can't handle the fact that your sister has a se—"

He held up his hand. "No more! You're right; I can't handle it. And on that note, I've got work to do." He bent down, gave Liv a quick kiss on the cheek, then turned to Imani. "Nice work today." She gave him a nod, and he turned and strode out.

Will grabbed my hand. "Come on. We've got some lounging to do." He made his doorway, and we stepped through into Angelica's reception room.

"Brrr, it's freezing in here." I hurried to the sitting room and magicked the fire into existence. Dizziness swirled in my skull. I gripped the mantle to keep from falling. Looked like we got home just in time.

"Are you okay?" Will's brow furrowed.

"Yep. Just used a bit too much magic today. After about twenty-four hours' sleep, I'll be fine." I grinned. "So, you promised me Indian."

He chuckled. "Hmm, so I did." He pulled out his phone and called Witcheroo. The food arrived within five minutes, just appearing on the dining-room table. We loaded up our plates, took them into the TV room, and sat on the couch. The news was on TV. "Oh, look, it's our favourite fortune teller." I growled. Stupid, arrogant, murdering idiot. Most of the non-witch world didn't know about us, but PIB arrests still made the news. The wider public just knew they were a special government agency, just not what, exactly.

Pure satisfaction calmed my nerves at the look of absolute hatred and anger on his face as he stood there in magic-blocking handcuffs. "Westerham's darling of the fortune-telling world has fallen about as far as one can go. He's been linked to numerous deaths, as it appears his talents were non-existent. Along with murder charges, he's been charged with fraud and obtaining money by deceptive practices. All his property and bank accounts have been seized."

Ha! It couldn't have happened to a nicer person. As bad as the last couple of weeks had been, we'd ended with a good outcome. One horrible person was dead, two others were in jail, and my friends were all alive and well, except for poor Gus, who was going to be scarred for life after what happened to his boss. We'd just have to make sure to convince him it wasn't his fault. And Liv wasn't going to jail. I smiled.

"Lily, look!" Will placed his plate on the floor and went to the multi-paned window that faced the front garden.

"What is it?" Oh God, not something else. Hadn't we had enough drama for one day? Actually, I'd had enough for a lifetime, but since we hadn't found my parents or put the snake group out of action, I was in for a hell of a lot more.

"Come here. You'll want to see this." He had his back to me, staring out the window, but his voice held joy rather than angst.

I jumped up and joined him. He slid his arm around me, and I burrowed into his side.

He dropped his voice, and his words flowed over me like a soft blanket. "Look. It's snowing."

Oh my God, so it was! I gasped in wonder at the white flakes floating silently to the ground. My heart swelled with excitement and reverence. A tingle of Will's power caressed my scalp, and the TV shut off. We stood in the dark, in the quiet, observing the ethereal beauty of Mother Nature at her peaceful best. Each flake was like a tiny, weightless fairy performing an ageless ballet. Had my parents ever stood here and watched it snow? My heart both ached with melancholy and swelled with love. I missed them so much, but I was thankful for the time we'd had together, and now I had more love from so many people. A tear tracked down my cheek, and I slid my arm around Will.

He turned me to face him and slipped his other arm around my back. "So, the universe granted you your wish." He smiled down at me.

"It sure did. Maybe it's not quite as mean as I thought."

"It better be nice to you; it has me to answer to if it's not." He leaned down and placed his lips on mine.

Okay, so maybe the universe and I were going to be friends after all. At least until next time....

ABOUT THE AUTHOR

USA Today bestselling author, Dionne Lister is a Sydneysider with a degree in creative writing, two Siamese cats, and is a member of the Science Fiction and Fantasy Writers of America. Daydreaming has always been her passion, so writing was a natural progression from staring out the window in primary school, and being an author was a dream she held since childhood.

Unfortunately, writing was only a hobby while Dionne worked as a property valuer in Sydney, until her mid-thirties when she returned to study and completed her creative writing degree. Since then, she has indulged her passion for writing while raising two children with her husband. Her books have attracted praise from Apple iBooks and have reached #1 on Amazon and iBooks charts worldwide, frequently occupying top 100 lists in fantasy. She's excited to add cozy mystery to the list of genres she writes. Magic and danger are always a heady combination.